The Book of Anne

The Story of the Childhood of Jesus
as told by His Grandmother

Charolette,

Peace be with you.
Sandy Ericson
2013

A Historical Novel by Sandy Martin Ericson

In memory of Charles and John

Prologue

Historians tell us the father of Mary was a successful Galilean farmer named Joachim. Most first century farmers lived in villages and worked small, nearby pieces of land. Like the farmer in the "Parable of the Prodigal Son," Joachim is thought to have owned large fields in a fertile valley in the Nazarean hills. Many parables spoken by Jesus were agricultural in nature. It is reasonable to presume he spent time amid wheat and sheep.

Scripture tells us the holy family journeyed from exile in Egypt to Galilee, rather than returning to Judea.

This story is of the life of Jesus during his childhood years and of his family and the people around him. It is a combination of history, geography, tradition, myth and imagination.

This then is how it might have been. Turn the page and imagine with me.

Sandy Martin Ericson

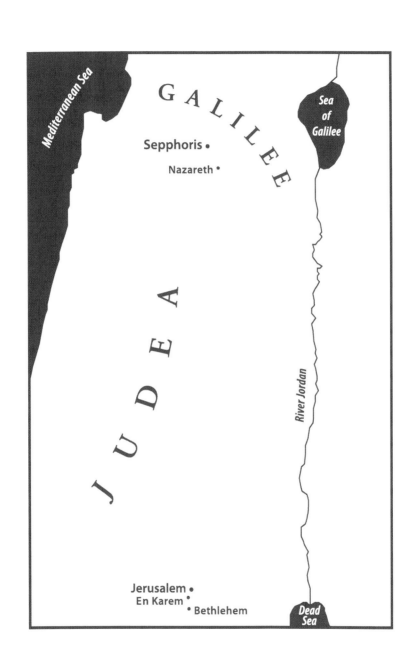

CHAPTER ONE: THE SCHOLAR

Thirty-Four Years After His Birth

A man came to Nazareth seeking a scribe. The Rabbi who taught lessons at the village school recommended Laban. Laban's father readily agreed. The reputation of the house of Joses was such that he felt no concern sending his only son to them. He welcomed the unexpected income.

Laban lived with his parents and sisters in a crowded room over his father's shop in the village of Nazareth. When not studying, eating or sleeping, he labored at his father's side, sweat dripping from his forehead as he stirred the clay or worked the potter's wheel. Though he did not entirely object to the work, neither did he object to this reprieve.

Laban happily greeted the opportunity to leave the village and walk the road winding through the hills on its way from Jerusalem to Sepphoris. Men sent by the house of Joses had come for him that morning. He had waited at his father's gate long before they arrived. He did not mind that they were quiet men who had no need of conversation.

They were not long upon the road before Laban felt a world away from the house of his father. The winter rains were over, but the road was not yet so dry as to raise dust beneath his feet. He walked beside sloping, green meadows where long-haired, fat-tailed sheep grazed amid bright clusters of saffron crocus. Birds sang sweetly from their hidden nests.

When the road made a sharp turn, Laban saw – spread out at the foot of a broad hill – a narrow valley lined with neat rows of wheat ready for harvest. He breathed in an intoxicating aroma rising from wild jasmine bushes growing at the corners of these cultivated plots.

At Laban's right, a stand of olive trees climbed a hill. Thickly leafing grape vines snaked between the trees and curled around their trunks. Hardy weeds with sharp thorns tangled with tall grasses at the edge of the road.

The boy was shocked when the men turned, and with a wave of their hands indicated that he should disappear with them into the thicket. One man held back a shrub revealing a faint path. When Laban stepped past, the man let the bush fly back into position, hiding the road from the path as cleverly as the path hid from the road.

Laban followed the men up the steep and gradually widening path. His heart beat wildly in his chest. What place was he being taken to that required such secrecy? When the three stepped into a clearing, Laban's misgivings were only slightly allayed by the welcoming scent of simmering barley broth and the aroma of baking bread.

Before him rose a courtyard wall the color of the hill. In its large, square opening stood a full-waisted woman with unruly, graying curls that refused to stay hidden beneath her scarf. A wide smile spread across her face. "Welcome to the house of Joses," said Sarah.

CHAPTER TWO: MOTHER ANNE

Thirty-four Years After His Birth

Anne sat on a garden chair made for her many years earlier by the husband of her daughter. He sculpted it from a great cedar trunk and rubbed it smooth with sandstone. She was grateful now to have its curving back to lean sideways against. She was happy that Sarah, wife of Joses the eldest grandson of her long-dead husband, had taken the burden of running this large and ever-growing household.

She smiled, thinking of the children she had seen born and nurtured there. She had watched the sons and grandsons of Joachim raise their children in the hill. "The hill is large and generous. Thanks be to the Lord God of Abraham," she said without realizing she had spoken aloud.

As she waited for the scholar from Nazareth, she thought of what lay ahead. The idea came from James. He sent a message that a young man would be coming. He insisted that while her mind remained keen she should tell the story of the years Mary, Joseph, and Jesus lived among them. He said the story must be written.

A frown formed on her face. She had not wanted to do this. Not all memories are meant to be shared. Some are best left to lie fallow. It had been a secret well kept. Why now need it be revealed? Only after a promise made to her by Joses did Anne agree to speak with the scholar.

She bent her head to follow her fine sewing. As the ivory needle flashed white in the sunlight filtering into her garden, Anne considered how she would begin her story. When she heard the gate latch click, she looked up from her musings. She saw that Sarah entered the garden, followed by a tall young man.

"Mother Anne, the scholar from Nazareth has arrived. He has been given drink and bread. His name is Laban." Saying nothing more Sarah returned to the courtyard leaving Laban standing at the garden gate.

"Peace be with you," greeted Anne as she gestured that he should come near.

"And also to you," Laban answered.

Anne liked what she saw. Black curls swirled above his broad forehead like a small dark cloud passing behind the sun. He looked strong and well fed. He dressed as if he had all that he needed. She watched him shift the weight of a roughly woven bag slung over his shoulder.

"Forgive me for not rising to greet you, but these old bones do not care to be often roused and cause a terrible ruckus within me should I move too swiftly." She saw Laban smile. It pleased her that he caught laughter in her voice, rather than complaint. It seemed to Anne that this boy might find listening to an old woman tolerable. But then, she reasoned, how might it not be tolerable having one's heaviest task the avoidance of slumber? With a nod toward his bag Anne asked, "What have you borne on such a long journey?"

"It is skin, brush and ink I carry."

"Ah, yes. That would be so." A sigh traveled from her heart to her lips. She shrugged and pointed to the ground near her chair. "Settle yourself as comfortably as you can. Not often do I have a chance to speak with a stranger. I fear when given one, I take full advantage."

Laban carefully lowered his bag from his shoulder to the ground at the spot Anne approved. He squatted and pulled at the drawstrings.

From the opened bag he first withdrew a rolled, pale gray dried goatskin scraped clean of hair. He spread the skin on the ground before him. Next he pulled from the sack a fat clay bottle sealed with mud and wrapped in cloth. He unwrapped the ink pot and broke the seal. With cautious precision he placed the ink pot and the cloth on the ground next to the skin.

From the folds of his tunic, Laban retrieved a polished stick. At one end the jet black hairs cut from the head of his elder sister made the stick a brush. Into the ink pot he dipped the homemade writing tool. Leaning forward, Laban slowly wrote upon the skin these words: The Book of Anne.

Laban raised his eyes and smiled.

Anne spoke with a sternness that surprised Laban. "You must make promises before we begin. You must promise that you will record with integrity all that I say, though there will be much that you will question."

"So be it," he promised.

"You must keep quiet your doubts."

"So be it," he repeated.

"You must promise to take no mind of tears which may fall unbidden from my eyes. I have lived long and well but none escapes misfortune. I have made peace with all, yet pain will not release his grip upon my heart. You must forgive an old woman her tears. Do not be burdened by them."

"So be it," he lied, surprised by a sudden urge to offer a comforting embrace to this frail, old woman.

Seeing concern in his face, Anne allowed her voice to soften. "Laban, you may call me Mother Anne, as do all who sleep beneath our roof."

She straightened in her chair and resumed her sewing. "James, the grandson of my husband and his wife before me, says I am to tell you the story in my own words. Thus, I have chosen to begin this tale with the greatest joy and surprise of my life, my wonderful Mary.

"I was barren far too long." Anne leaned toward Laban, her voice nearly a whisper. "I would not speak of it now, for I honor the memory of my husband. Yet, I cannot fully tell of Mary if I keep secret how she came to be borne by my womb."

Laban stared hard at the ground. A blush rushed up his neck and onto his face. The widow of the revered, deceased, farmer Joachim had hinted of scandal. This he could not record.

"Mother Anne," Laban asked, trying not to let his voice reveal his shock. "Yes?"

"Please have no offense if I put away my writing tools. Perhaps I must listen carefully and think long before I put pen to skin."

"Ah, you are both clever and prudent." Anne was pleased with his suggestion. "You are correct. Much of this story I have seen with my own eyes. Much of this story I have heard from the lips of others. You must take from my ramblings that which will be of use. I regret I cannot speak in beautifully formed sentences. I will leave such sculpting to you. Put away your writing tools and lie back and listen. When our ears tire of my voice, you may retire elsewhere to write that of my story you find worthy of ink and skin."

Laban carefully returned to the bag all but the skin upon which he had written. This he left spread upon the ground so that the ink could fully dry. He sat cross-legged to the left of Anne. He could not bring himself to lie back.

Anne forgot her sewing as she began to speak, "The story begins here, in this garden."

CHAPTER THREE: A BLESSING ON THE HOUSE OF JOACHIM

Fifteen Years Before His Birth

As his ancestors roaming the desert added rooms to their tents when sons took wives, Joachim added rooms in the hill.

At the time Joachim took Anne as wife, David, his first-born, had brought his wife Marta to the hill and added two sons of his own to the house. Joachim's grown daughter Ester remained in his house, as well as Jude and Jacob, his younger sons born by his second wife.

If Anne missed her father's house, no one knew of it, for she gave herself completely to Joachim and his family.

In the beginning, Joachim's adult children were careful to respect Anne's position as wife of their father. Soon they forgot their caution and were as much in love with her as was their father. The children of the house adored her without hesitation and often sought solace in her warm embrace.

When a second tilling passed with no bulge in Anne's belly, Ester and Marta went about their daily tasks silently begging the Lord God of Abraham to bless Anne with child.

They knew not that age robbed Joachim of his stamina and it was he who carried the pain of Anne's barren womb. Anne worried not. "It is the Lord's doing," she told her husband. "Have not you already fathered a fine family? This land will be farmed forever by your descendents. For what more would you ask?"

When Joachim protested that it was not for his but for her happiness he was concerned, Anne laughed. "See you not these children around me? You have given me many to love. Worry not."

In the early afternoon of a spring day Ester, Marta and the children lay napping on pallets in cool rooms.

In her sun-washed garden, Anne sat crossed-legged on a rug spread on the ground. A bit of unfinished sewing perched untouched on her knee as she enjoyed the quiet.

"Anne," she heard whispered. She looked around, but saw no one. She wondered, had she fallen asleep and dreamed a voice? She shook her head, picked up the sewing and searched for the bone needle pinned to the cloth.

A breeze swept through the garden causing newly sprouted plants to touch frail tops to the ground. "Anne."

She shivered and called out, "Who would speak with me?"

Before her, wrapped in a brilliant, white light, appeared a great angel with wide, sweeping, translucent wings.

Anne's eyes grew round. Her mouth flew open and her body shook. Her breath froze and pushed hard at her chest as she cried out, "My mind is lost!"

Anne heard a whisper. "Do not be afraid. Rejoice and be glad. You carry a girl child who will be blessed among all women." The angel's voice swirled around her like a warm summer wind. She moved her hands across her belly. Joy replaced fear.

The light and the angel grew faint.

"Wait, wait, go not," she begged and rose as if to chase after the angel. A thick mist formed around her and held her in place. "What is this? What is happening to me?" Anne weakened and fainted, slipping to the ground as if lowered by invisible, protective arms.

The angel vanished.

A water carrier raised the horn of a ram to his lips sending a plaintive call into the valley.

The men working amid the barley lay down sickles, wiped sweat from their faces and waited for Joachim to lead them in prayer before they took their rest.

With the skirt of his tunic tucked into his girdle, Joachim kneeled in a row of wheat at the edge of the road. His obedient and patient donkey Asia stood nearby.

Pleased that he saw no sign of wheat rot, Joachim stood and shouted thanks, "Praise be to the Lord God of Abraham." The wheat shoot in his hands fell to the ground. A paralysis gripped him. Words could no longer escape his throat. He feared he had been too long in the sun. He wondered if he were dying.

As quickly as a mouse slips from stalk to stalk, a fully formed sentence slipped into his head. "You are Abraham. Go to your Sarah."

A shudder ran though Joachim releasing his paralysis as abruptly as it had come upon him. He leapt upon Asia and whipped her into action. The startled animal brayed as she bolted. Joachim wrapped his arms around her neck, buried his face in her short, stiff mane and held tight.

With mouths agape, the stunned field workers watched until Joachim and Asia followed the curve of the road and disappeared from their sight.

They gathered in a circle and found their voices. Some said they should follow Joachim. David said his father would not wish them to leave the barley on a day so well meant for reaping.

In the end they did both. Those who stayed felt righteous for tending the soil and the future of the house of Joachim. Those who hurried away believed they served a sacred mission to rescue their benefactor from the disaster into which he surely must be riding.

The voice called so faintly Anne was not certain it was her name she heard. She felt a soft breeze upon her cheeks. She heard her name again and wondered who had such desperate need of her?

A shock of cold at her temples brought her awake. She found herself in the arms of Marta who stroked Anne's temples with a damp cloth. Ester knelt beside them fanning the air with a bundle of reeds.

"Dear Mother Anne, how do you feel?" Marta asked when she saw that Anne had awakened.

"Like a child in your arms. How did this happen?" Anne struggled to sit.

"We found you lying here. You must have fainted. Are you hurt?"

Anne thought of her body. "No, no. I think no harm has come to me. How foolish."

Ester and Marta exchanged knowing glances and repressed smiles.

Anne remembered the words so sweetly spoken. "You carry a girl child who will be blessed among all women." She grinned and then laughed. "Help me up. Have we missed the prayers? Has the whole household seen me lying here?"

"Mother Anne, the prayers can wait. As to the household, I believe this one has need for rejoicing. We have much for which to thank our Lord God of Abraham, is this not so?" Marta asked as she helped Anne rise to her feet.

Anne composed herself, but could not resist placing a hand upon her stomach. Instinct told her to speak not of the angel. "Daughters, not a word to any. I have not yet told Joachim. It is right that he be told before the others."

"The secret shall be kept." Marta promised.

Ester saw that Jacob and Jude stood whispering by the garden gate. She frowned and waved her hand behind Anne signaling her young brothers to leave. In a loud voice, she said, "Dear Mother Anne, we rejoice that you are well."

Marta helped Anne straighten her tunic. "Perhaps the sun was stronger than you thought and has had an ill affect upon you. What harm might come from enjoying a small rest in the cool of the hill?"

"I have rested enough this day." Anne protested.

Marta and Ester pulled Anne from her garden, through the courtyard, and into the room in the hill Anne shared with Joachim.

They had barely left Anne upon her pallet when a commotion began in the clearing. An ewe bleated and chickens squawked. Ester called back through the slatted door. "It is Joachim."

Anne caught her breath. She had not considered how to share this good news with her husband. What if Joachim did not believe that an angel came? Her heart froze in her chest. Would he throw her from his house? She trembled at the sound of his sandals slapping against the courtyard floor.

Joachim yanked open the latticed door, nearly pulling it from the hinges. He burst into the room and threw himself at the feet of his wife. His body shook, tears streamed from his eyes, "Anne," he beseeched, "tell me, it is so."

Anne felt weak, but managed to raise Joachim to his feet. She used the edge of her sleeve to dry his tears. "Dear Husband, of what do you speak?"

"Oh my wife! A voice came to me and drove me here. It said I am Abraham and you are my Sarah. Can this mean you are with child?"

"My beloved husband, it is so." She told him of the angel, of the light and of the girl child in her womb. She told him that Marta and Ester had found her lying in faint.

Joachim pulled away.

Anne watched as he walked to the far side of the room, turned and walked back to her. In the dim room she could not see which emotions traveled across his face. Her fears returned. Food roiled in her stomach. She bowed her head.

The noise of the field workers being greeted and then hushed reached Anne and Joachim. They paid it no heed.

Finally Joachim spoke. "Did others see the angel deliver this news?"

"I think not. All were resting. I was alone in the garden."

"Do not mistake me, wife, I honor this girl child in your womb. We have been spoken to. The others have not. The child must be protected. Let us keep to ourselves that an angel delivered this good news."

"So be it, husband," Anne promised with great relief that her husband believed her words.

Wrapping his arms around Anne, Joachim gently lowered her to the ground. They sat on the hard packed dirt, she in his embrace. "I felt this, Anne. I felt this in the field. For a moment, I thought I had gone mad."

Anne leaned her head upon his shoulder. "This is good. Is it not?"

"This news has come to me in a way that makes my head spin like dust in a drought. I know not what to make of it." He sighed.

Rejoicing in Joachim's acceptance of the miracle presented to them, Anne felt strong. "Husband, Yahweh will reveal all that we must know. Let us be glad."

Anne and Joachim heard Asia bray as if beset by bees. They both laughed.

"I am surprised the old girl has the energy to sneeze after that flight up this hill. You should have seen her run. You should have seen me! I held on with all my might, so great was my fear that I should find myself flying off her back and rolling downward with such force as to send the whole hill racing down after me."

Anne laughed.

Joachim hugged her. He stood and helped her rise. "Come, we have good news for an old man to share."

The couple entered the courtyard. Joachim cried out, "Sound the Shofar. Call all in from the fields. Slaughter a lamb. Tonight we feast. The Lord God of Abraham has again blessed this household. A child is to be born."

Shouts of happiness rose to the sky. Jude climbed a ladder and stood atop the courtyard wall. He raised the ram's horn to his lips and sent a happy call to the men who remained in the fields.

Marta waved Anne away from the fire and took charge of preparations. She sent the boys in search of eggs hidden in the brush. She ordered the men out of the way of the women. "Make music," she told them.

Joachim sent Jacob to fetch a lamb from his flock and set about building a spit upon which to turn it. Ester worked to build up the fire.

A flute began to sing.

CHAPTER FOUR: REBEKAH

Thirty-four Years Following His Birth

Remembering the joy of the day she and Joachim had been spoken to, Anne grew quiet. For the moment, she forgot the scholar.

Laban welcomed Anne's silence for he had much to consider. He believed in angels. The scripture spoke of them. He had never before known a person who spoke of being visited by one. He was not certain how to receive this information.

Laban saw that Anne's eyes betrayed a mind that was far away from where they sat. He thought of his own grandmother who, in her final years, often seemed lost and unsure of the people around her, and who often spoke of things unseen by others. He remembered the kindness with which his mother and father treated her. Perhaps the recording of this tale was merely an indulgence by a loving family?

The latch clicked and gate swung open. Anne and Laban were startled out of their musings and both turned toward the gate. Anne spoke. "Ah, Rebekah, what brings you into the garden?"

Spellbound by the beauty of the girl who walked toward him, Laban did not realize that he had risen to his feet. *Perhaps*, he thought, *angels do visit this garden.*

The daughter and youngest child of Joses and Sarah moved with grace. She was slender and nearly as tall as Laban. Her long, dark brown hair fell in waves down to her shoulders. Water splashed from the two wooden bowls she carried.

"Mother Anne, it is drink I bring. My mother sent me." Rebekah grinned and said, "She wondered if your lips had grown dry having been so long in use." She laughed and gave Anne a cup and turned toward Laban. "Peace be with you," she said as she extended the cup to him.

Laban's tongue seemed stuck to the roof of his mouth. He was

21

barely able to loosen it to offer thanks when Rebekah presented the water. "And also you," he croaked.

Anne looked at Laban, at Rebekah and back to Laban. A smile hinted at the edges of her lips for she saw that Laban looked at Rebekah as Joseph had looked at her Mary when he first saw that she had become a woman. She also noted that Rebekah seemed unable to look directly at the lad. "Child, do you wish to sit with us? I am certain our scholar here would not object to your presence."

Laban felt a blush rush up his neck. He knew not what to say. He was shocked that Anne would ask the girl to sit with him, a stranger. He sipped from the cup, but he could not turn his eyes away from Rebekah.

Rebekah turned to Anne, her voice steady, her composure belying her inner turmoil, "Mother Anne, my mother has sent me to inquire whether you are in need of rest."

"No dear one. Now that I have begun speaking, I find I enjoy an audience. Come for me when the sun has reached its highest point in the sky."

"So be it," Rebekah replied. She turned without saying more. Aware that Laban stared after her, she forced herself to slowly walk from the garden.

Reminded of new love's charm, Anne wanted to laugh aloud. Instead, she directed Laban, "Scholar, make yourself comfortable. The water has refreshed my tongue."

Laban had not quite settled on the ground when Anne took up her story.

"Mary was a wonderful child. She must have cried as an infant. Truly I do not recall that she did. She walked and spoke long before do most. She was a loving child. She was hardly tall enough to reach the end of my sleeve when she begged to help me with my chores.

"Ah, so beautiful! Her hair – dark at birth – paled and then turned dark again. I loved to brush her thick curls and tie them with ribbons my husband bought from the caravan merchants passing by his fields."

Laban pictured his mother brushing the dark hair of his younger sister. It was a pretty sight.

"Mary played, always in my presence. Though the entire household delighted in her, and no doubt we were overly forgiving of her, she remained sweet and unspoiled."

Anne was quiet a moment, savoring her memories. When she spoke again a yearning for days past sounded in her voice, "She loved to visit the market in Sepphoris. I can see her now tracing her tiny hands along the rolls of silk. Her favorite task was to search among the fruit spread out on the rugs. She seemed always to find the unblemished pear.

"When it was time, I taught her all that a woman should know." Anne paused, her eyes filled with sadness. She sighed and whispered, "It seemed she had hardly been with us."

CHAPTER FIVE: A PROMISE MADE

Two Years Before His Birth

In the brilliant blue, nearly cloudless sky, a sparrow hawk carefully trolled for mice above harvested fields. Forty feet below and following the crooked road, a donkey cart bumped along, stirring up dust clouds.

The driver searched ahead for the turn-off that would lead up through a thick olive grove. There he would leave Joseph and continue with his load of geese borne for market in Sepphoris.

The carpenter Joseph sat with legs dangling from the back of the cart, his feet brushing the road. He watched the hawk float, wheel and dive. He wished somehow he could be up there soaring along looking down upon the earth with sharp eyes. Lost in his daydreams, he nearly fell from the cart when it shuddered to a sudden stop.

"Alight," the driver called back to him.

Joseph jumped to the ground and collected a bag, heavy with the weight of his rule, plane and ax. He slung the bag over his shoulder and walked to the side of the cart. From a pocket in his tunic he pulled a bronze coin. "Many thanks for speeding my journey. May you continue in peace," he said as he offered payment.

The driver bit the coin to verify its authenticity. Satisfied, he hid it in the folds of the girdle at his waist. "The house of Joachim leans into the center of the hill. It is an easy climb," he said and urged the donkey on, leaving Joseph standing in the settling dust.

The carpenter turned away from the grain fields. Before him a broad path snaked upward. Though not as heavily traveled as the road the cart followed, the path was wide and he could see that an oxen-pulled cart could find its way up the hill.

He left the road and followed the path. Soon sweat dampened his forehead, causing his long hair to cling to his narrow face. He was not an old man, nor was he young. He was strong, yet at times, the steepness of the path forced him to put down his bag and rest under the shade of the olive trees edging its sides.

He knew his effort would be rewarded, for this was the house of an old friend who was known as a great and generous farmer whose table was always set.

When he saw Ester standing upon the path, he knew he had reached the clearing. "Peace be with you," he called out.

"And also with you. Welcome again to my father's house," Ester answered and gestured that Joseph should follow. She led him past the goats and chickens and into the courtyard terraced into the side of the hill.

Joseph straightened to his full height when he noticed upon him the eyes of a young woman. Joachim's daughter Mary stood by the well dressed in a tunic the color of the sky.

Her beauty startled Joseph. Her thick, black hair, tied with a piece of cloth at the nape of her neck fell to her waist. Her skin was smooth and her features delicate. Joseph could see that dark brown eyes sparkled beneath full lashes. *Is this,* he asked himself, *the child I have seen playing at Mother Anne's feet?* He was surprised that the girl did not turn away, but remained still, watching him as he approached.

Anne – who sat at a loom – frowned at her daughter, but smiled inwardly. She was not so old that she could not remember the thrill of a guest's arrival. "Tend to the water, Mary," she reminded.

Anne rose from her work and walked to Joseph. "Welcome to this house. My husband will be full of regret when he learns that he was not here to greet you. He has promised to return soon and would not be absent if it were not for some urgent work in the fields. You must wash and eat, or God will punish me for being inhospitable. This you would not wish upon me."

Anne returned to her loom. Ester led Joseph to a tan and black striped rug spread upon the hard packed ground. Next to the rug Mary placed a large, shallow clay bowl and a pale drying-cloth.

Joseph sat on the rug and unlaced his sandals. He was thrilled when Mary brought water in a gourd and poured it over his hands outstretched above the bowl. He dared not look at her lovely face as he washed his hands.

Joseph used the water that fell into the bowl to wash his feet. He dried his hands and feet. When he completed the washing, he looked up at Mary. He was shocked to find no words would form on his lips, nor would any sound come from his throat.

Without speaking, Mary took away the cloth and the bowl. Her face was solemn but laughter danced in her eyes. She did not understand the reason, but she knew that Joseph's discomfort pleased her.

Ester came with a thin round of flatbread and a small bowl filled with broth.

Joseph stood to receive the food. He stepped onto the rug. Yahweh released his tongue. "I thank the Lord my God for the food which he has given me. Amen." Without glancing at the women around him, Joseph sat upon the rug and ate.

Ester and Mary stood behind him so that he should not dine alone. Ester wished that he would eat quickly, for she had much work to do. Mary hoped that he would linger over his meal so that she could study him without his knowing. She saw that his broad shoulders pulled his tunic tight across his back. She had already noted that he had good teeth and was quick to smile. Something stirred in her she had never before felt.

Joseph folded the flatbread, using it to scoop up the generous serving of thick barley broth dotted with bits of lamb. As he ate, he felt he was seeing the house of Joachim for the first time.

Before him, to his left, snug against the curved courtyard wall, stairs led to an enclosed upper room jutting out from the hill with a wooden door and a shuttered window. The upper room served as a roof for a corner room beneath it.

The lower corner room had two sides open to the courtyard, braced where they met by a thick, square column of mud bricks. Sheltered there were clay pots, pitchers and bowls. He saw iron plates for roasting grain, a mortar and wheel for grinding and a stack of clay saucers and wicks. Large earthen jars holding oils and grains stood in a row against the hill.

Before this room a fire pit had been dug. Upon the embers sat tall earthen pots holding the simmering and aromatic barley broth. Like perfect circles etched by the stick of a potter, rounds of flatbreads baked on the sides of the cooking vessels.

Between the open corner room and the beginning of a row of latticed doors leading to rooms in the hill, a fully leafed fig tree partly obscured a small gate. Joseph watched a sparrow hop among the branches.

He wiped the bowl clean and swallowed the last bite of bread. He laced on his sandals and again stood to pray. "Lord, you have blessed me with the food of this household. I thank you and the house of Joachim. Amen."

All in the courtyard turned at the sound of a donkey's bray. They heard Joachim's laughter before he appeared in the opening of the courtyard wall. He stopped there, holding the end of the rope looped around Asia's neck.

Mary ran to him and took the donkey's lead from him. Joachim kissed the sides of his daughter's face. "Ah, my lovely one, thank you. Take the poor old girl to water."

Sitting at the loom, Anne watched the eyes of Joseph follow Mary.

Joachim strode into the courtyard, his arms extended in greeting. "Joseph, Joseph, my friend. Forgive me for not being here to greet you. Have you been here long? Was your journey safe? Has my wife taken good care of you? Have you been fed?"

The men embraced and kissed each other's faces.

"The house of Joachim is generous. I have been well cared for," Joseph assured his host.

"This is good." Joachim laughed. "Wife, Joseph and I will sit in your garden. Ask Mary to draw water for us." He grabbed two rugs from a stack near Anne, bending down to kiss the face of his wife as he passed her loom.

"Come Joseph. Let us go into the garden. I am anxious to hear what news you bring from the great city of Jerusalem." He threw the rugs over his shoulder and grabbed Joseph by the hand, pulling him to the small gate behind the fig tree.

Joseph joined Joachim's laughter. He was pleased and honored that Joachim had left the fields to greet him.

Joachim dropped Joseph's hand and pushed open the gate. He held open the gate so that Joseph could pass beneath an arch of ancient grapevines. Joachim followed and dropped the rugs on the ground. He spread one out flat and patted it with an open palm. "Sit here, my friend."

Joseph obeyed and sat crossed legged upon the rug with his back to Anne's patch of carefully tended vegetables and herbs.

Joachim threw the second rug on the ground in front of Joseph and squatted upon it. "So, Joseph, thank you for the generosity of your visit." He put a finger to his lips and whispered. "I have asked you here to build a gift for my wife. I have not yet revealed this to her."

Joachim leaned in toward Joseph. "She thinks you come to make handles for our scythes and yokes for our plows." He laughed. "But, please, before we speak of your true work here, tell me what news bring you?"

Joseph smiled at his host. "It is good to walk in the fresh air of Galilee. It pleases me to once again be in your company. I am at your service. Please Joachim, tell me first of your family."

"Ah, Joseph, the hill continues to collect people! Ora, wife of my son Jacob, has blessed this house with two sons since last you visited. Joses is the first-born. He walks and talks and begs to go to the fields. His brother,

James, is yet a hearty babe."

"Congratulations, Joachim. You are most fortunate. This house is blessed with many sons."

"The Lord God of Abraham has been generous. But Joseph, tell me of life in the great city."

"The great city is crowded, Joachim. One can cross it and not touch the ground. I can leap from rooftop to rooftop from the northern to the southern wall. Yet Herod continues to build."

"This is good, is it not? There must be much work for a man such as you?"

"This is true. But I do not care for labor within the city walls. Herod's masters are harsh. Yet, one good has come of it."

"And this good would be?"

"Herod had need of the land upon which sat my father's house in the old, decaying area of the city. Long ago, the Sanhedrin recorded the land as belonging to my family. Thus, I was given a fair price. With the money I have purchased a small plot in the area of the gardens outside the northernmost wall. The air is clean there. Already I have a foundation in place."

"This is good news, indeed, Joseph. You have been most fortunate."

Both men turned at the sound of the gate opening. Mary entered, carrying two small bowls of water. She placed a bowl on the ground before Joseph. She did not allow her eyes to meet his. The second bowl she handed to her father.

"Ah, daughter, this is good." He turned to Joseph, pretending not to see that Joseph watched his daughter. "Our well is fed from a river hidden deep in the hill. It is pure and better even than Solomon's wines."

Joseph could not pull his eyes away from Mary. He had gone without a wife far longer than most men. More than one father had made it known to Joseph that he had a daughter ready for a marriage promise. He was glad now that he had resisted. He knew now that the daughter of Joachim was the woman for whom he had waited. "Thank you, my friend. I do thirst."

"Father, what more may I do for you?"

"This is good, daughter. You may return to your sewing."

"Thank you, father," Mary said and left the garden.

Joseph watched Mary until she disappeared beyond the gate.

"Joseph. Joseph?"

Joseph felt a flush creep up his neck and onto his cheeks. Had Joachim read his thoughts? He brushed an imaginary twig from the rug upon which he sat. "Joachim, please tell me of this work you wish me to do."

A smile edging Joachim's lips became a grin. "Joseph, you are known to plane a tree limb smooth and frame a room square. I have also heard that you do more than most carpenters. I have heard that you also are a maker of tables and chairs. Is this not so?"

"Yes. I have done so."

"I have found in a field a great cedar tree. Its trunk is thick as the belly of a cow ready to give birth. Am I foolish to think that it may be made into a chair for my Anne to use to sit in the shade of her garden?"

"A bench would not require such a piece of wood."

"I do not wish for you to build a bench. I wish for you to build a chair with a smooth back and high sides, so that when my wife is old, she can lean against it and think of when she was young."

Joseph was thoughtful, having never considered building a chair in this way. He imagined such a thing possible. "I must see this great piece of wood. I would not wish to promise to do such a task without knowing that I could accomplish it."

"So be it." Joachim stood. "Beyond this garden, a trail leads through the grove to a pasture where I have had my sons drag the old tree. Let us go there now, while the light is with us."

"Yes, let us." Joseph barely had time to rise from the rug before Joachim was disappearing into the grove.

Hava, the daughter of David, the eldest son of Joachim, was only a few months younger than Mary. Hava and Mary loved each other, as do sisters grown in one womb. They played together. They worked together. One kept no secret from the other.

Hava sat on the ground using a mortar to grind barley grain for bread making. She looked up when she heard the click of the garden gate. She saw something different about Mary. Mary skipped, rather than walked. Her eyes smiled. Hava wondered what had brought this change?

Mary sat next to Hava. "May I be of help?" Mary took the bowl of grain and the mortar from Hava's hands.

"Mary, what is it?" Hava asked.

"Why, I only mean to help."

"No. What has happened? You do not seem yourself."

Mary turned her head so that Anne could not see the words forming on her lips. She nearly laughed as she whispered, "He is handsome."

Hava's eyes widened. "The carpenter? Why, sister. Your face reddens when you speak of him."

"Be quiet. Say no more."

Anne looked up from her loom and saw that the two young women huddled together. "Hava, have you no work to do? Come, stand by me and hold the wool."

Surrounded by a carpet of blue and white summer flowers, Joseph worked for a full cycle of the moon, refusing to leave his task until completed. He slept rolled in a rug on the ground. He ate and drank the food and water brought to him by Joachim's sons.

Joseph was captured by the scent of the wood that rose up when he shaved the bark from the trunk. With his axe he cut away a piece that stood from the ground to his waist. From this piece he sculpted the form of the chair. Its back and sides curved down from the center and leveled out to form shelves upon which Anne could rest her arms. In the lower half, he carved a thick seat and four stubby legs with feet that looked like garden toads bathing in sunlight. He spent hours carefully sanding and rubbing the chair. If someone approached, he was quick to cover his work, so that not even Joachim could know of its beauty.

From the remaining wood, he made a long, high, narrow table. This too he rubbed until it shone like polished marble.

When he was done, he covered them both and sent for Joachim.

Joachim arrived with a donkey cart and men from the field to load the chair into the cart. "Ah, Joseph," he shouted as he jumped from the cart. He left the men standing at the edge of the road and hurried into the field. "I am told your work here is done. This is a great day, is it not?"

The men embraced. "I know the sun shines and the air is fresh. This is a great day. Peace be with you my friend."

Joachim laughed. "Do not keep me longer in suspense. Let me see this work hiding here. Why do two forms stand beneath your blankets? Which of these is for my Anne?"

Joseph pulled away the cloth draped over the chair.

Joachim gaped at the gleaming wood. He moved to it and ran his hand across the smooth seat. "Joseph, I... uh, I have not words. This chair is more beautiful than any my mind could see." He stroked the chair arms.

Joseph saw that tears glistened in Joachim's eyes and threatened to spill down his face. "I am happy that my work pleases you."

Joachim recovered his composure. "You have, Joseph. You have. Now, what is covered by this other piece of wool?"

31

"Walk with me. This piece requires discussion."

Puzzled, Joachim could only reply, "So be it."

Together they walked beyond the beautiful chair to the piece still hidden. Joseph tugged at the corner of the cloth and let it fall away from the table. "In the city, the women use tables such as this to hold the cups and platters and cooking tools. Beneath it, they store vessels of grain, oil and wine."

"Joseph, this table seems too beautiful for such use."

"Thank you. You may use it as you wish. It is a gift, as is the chair."

"Gifts?"

"Yes." Joseph began to speak as if he had practiced the words. "You know that I am not a rich man, yet I do not lack for work. I own a plot of land in a desirable area near the gardens outside the walls of Jerusalem. Already I have begun building a house. Though simple, it will offer a secure refuge for a family."

A smile played at Joachim's lips as he told himself his Anne had been correct. Anne had assured him Joseph had fallen in love with Mary the moment he saw her at the well.

Joseph cleared his throat. Words rushed from his lips. "Sir, I wish to offer the table and chair as a dowry for my betrothal to your daughter Mary."

Though Joseph's words did not surprise him, Joachim found it difficult to speak. Mary was a woman. He and Anne had known that this day neared, yet it came too quickly.

Joseph's breathing stopped as he waited for Joachim's reply.

"Ah, my heart breaks at the thought of my sweet Mary living far from us. Yet, she is of age. I can think of no better man for her to live out her life. Before I agree to this marriage promise, you must promise that you will not allow her to disappear from our lives."

"Joachim, you have made me a happy man. I have long waited for a wife. I vow to seek many opportunities to find work in Galilee so that your daughter may often return to sleep in your house."

"Instruct the men who wait on the road of how to stow the table and chair in the cart." He sighed, thinking of Anne. "Let us hope that the beauty of your work will ease my wife's pain at the loss of her daughter."

"Your daughter is not lost. I will not break my promise."

"So be it." Joachim said, silently vowing to find much work for Joseph in the Nazarean hills.

CHAPTER SIX: THE GOOD NEWS

His First Year

The sun had not risen so high above the hills as to shine directly into the courtyard. The men had left for the fields. The women had cleared way the remnants of the morning meal and scattered to tend other chores.

Mary had finished shaking the sleeping rugs and was gathering them to take into the hill when she sensed she was no longer alone. She turned toward the open gate. A man stood there.

She could see that he was a large man who appeared strong. She could see that his hair and full beard were the color of snow. She could see that he was richly dressed.

The folds of his ivory tunic were thick. Its wide sleeves were long and hid all but the tips of his fingers. The hem of his garment fell to the ground and folded upon itself. Gold threads woven throughout the fabric of his mantle ended in a thick, glimmering fringe.

Surprised, but feeling no menace in the sudden appearance of this stranger, Mary greeted him. "Peace be with you."

"And also with you," the man answered, but he did not move into the courtyard.

"Sir, you are welcome to enter this house. May I bring you drink from the well? The water is cold and pure. It will refresh you after the long climb up this hill."

The man smiled. "No, Mary," he replied. "I have no need of water, nor of barley broth. The house of Joachim is generous, but I came not for sustenance."

Mary knew not what to think of such words. She bowed her head. "You know this family. Sir, forgive my ignorance, for I know you not. Please give me your name so that I may tell my father of your arrival."

"I am Gabriel. It is not Joachim I seek today. I am the angel Gabriel. It is you to whom I carry a message."

The rugs fell from Mary's hands. Her body shook. She felt weak and wished to flee, yet she stood held in place.

Gabriel stood before her. He raised his arms above her head, palms down in blessing. "I bring to you news of great joy. You carry in your womb the child of God, a son, the Messiah whom you will name Emmanuel."

Mary dropped to her knees. Overwhelmed, doubt filled her head with questions. *Does he say I carry the child of God? Our Messiah? The one for whom we have so long waited? I am the one? This cannot be. There can be no child in my womb. I am innocent.*

Mary opened her eyes, looked into the face of Gabriel, and saw that a brilliant light surrounded him. In that moment, she understood there was no choice. Yahweh had willed it. Lifting her arms to the angel, she bowed her head. "Behold, I am the handmaid of the Lord. May it be done to me according to your word."

Gabriel placed his hands upon Mary's head. The light coiled around her body and entered into her. "You carry in your womb the promised savior, the Messiah. He will be great. He will be called Son of the Most High and the Lord God. His kingdom will live forever. God has chosen you to bear his son in fulfillment of the scriptures. You are blessed among all women."

He raised her to her feet.

Mary felt calm and once again looked into the face of Gabriel. The light was gone. He appeared as he had standing at the gate. Drawing on courage that surprised her, she asked, "Oh, great angel, how is it that I carry a child? How can this be, as I have not been with man?"

The angel laughed and whispered, "All things are possible with God." He grew serious and began to instruct Mary. "You are to go to Judea to the house of Zechariah. Your cousin Elizabeth is in her sixth month. She too bears a son who, at the right time, will announce the coming of the Messiah. The son of Elizabeth will be called John the Baptizer."

"So be it," Mary answered. She felt the air cool as a shadow passed over the courtyard. In an instant, the pink light of early morning returned.

Mary saw that the angel was no longer with her. She let her hands linger over her belly. She found a rug and lay down upon it. Savoring her gift, she covered herself with her mantle and lay still.

CHAPTER SEVEN: A PROMISE KEPT

His First Year

Thinking her daughter was taking an unusually long time shaking the rugs, Anne went into the courtyard. When she saw Mary lying on the ground, she was alarmed. "Daughter, why lie you there? What harm has come to you?"

Mary pulled aside her mantel, sat up and smiled. She spoke with authority. "Mother, you must now prepare for my leaving. I am to go to my cousin Elizabeth."

Anne was stunned. "What for my daughter bears such urgency that she should so order me?"

Mary rose and embraced her mother. Grasping Anne's hands, she stepped back and explained. "A great angel named Gabriel came to me as I was working here in the courtyard."

"Who came here?"

"Mother, an angel came. The angel Gabriel! He says I bear the child of God. Even now as we speak, I feel a stirring in my womb. It is true. I am with child, a male child. We are to name him Emmanuel. Mother, this babe is the Messiah we have long awaited."

Anne remembered the words so softly spoken in her garden filled with bright light. "You are with child. A girl child who will be blessed among women." She trembled. Dread engulfed her. Her daughter would not have the protection she had enjoyed of living in the house of her husband before she was with child.

Mary's voice became urgent. "Mother, the angel has instructed me to go to Elizabeth. He says she is heavy with child. I must go and be with her as her time nears."

"Elizabeth? Elizabeth? Elizabeth with child? She is long past her childbearing years. Never have I heard such nonsense from you." Anne placed the back of her hand on the forehead of her daughter. "Have you a fever?"

Mary laughed and quoted Gabriel. "All things are possible with God." A grin filled her face.

She tried to pull her mother toward the lattice door that led to their room. "Come, we have much to do. The angel instructed me to go to my cousin for she is in need of my care. Truly, she carries a son. His name is to be John."

Anne resisted Mary and lowered herself onto a crumpled rug. In her mind, she heard the words of Joachim: "We have been spoken to."

That an angel had come to her daughter, she did not doubt. That her daughter carried the Son of God, she did not doubt. That Joachim would understand the message, she did not doubt. That Elizabeth carried a child? This she doubted.

Anne thought of Joseph. Dread filled her. What might he make of this? She wished that Yahweh had not given them the burden of delivering this message to Mary's betrothed. Aloud she said, "Mary, must not we first tell Joseph of this?"

Mary gasped, raising her hand to her mouth. "Oh, yes, yes. How thoughtless of me. Can Papa send for Joseph at this hour?"

Anne's eyes filled with worry.

"Mother, do not be concerned. Yahweh is with us."

"So be it," Anne answered with a confidence she did not feel.

On the sixth day, as the light left and the dark filled the sky, Joachim lit a lamp and waited near the gate. Anne and Mary waited behind the latticed door. Mary fell asleep, leaning against her mother.

Anne worried that Joseph would not be able to accept the tale of a visit by an angel. She held her daughter's hand and silently prayed to the Lord God of Abraham that Joseph would be as good to Mary as Joachim has been to her.

When she heard Joachim call out, Anne shook Mary awake. Anne put her fingers over her daughter's lips warning her to speak not.

Joachim called out, "Joseph, is it you?"

"It is I. The boy says you have urgent need of me. What is it that requires that I abandon my labors?"

Joachim told the boy, "Put up the animals. Feed and water them before you rest." To Joseph he said, "Come and sit with me near the coals. There we will talk."

From behind the slats, Mary and Anne watched the shadowy figures of Joachim and Joseph move to a rug spread near the dying embers in the fire pit. Anne was not surprised that her husband forgot his manners and began to speak without offering food or drink. She and Joachim were filled with apprehension. Only Mary seemed calm in this matter.

The men sat with their heads bent close. Joachim spoke so softly the women could not hear his words.

Anne shuddered when they heard a sorrowful keening such as a new widow makes when she throws herself upon the coffin of her husband.

They heard Joachim cry out, "Joseph! Do not leave us." They heard the sound of Joseph's feet hitting the hard packed dirt. They heard Joachim fall upon the ground and wail.

Mary and Anne ran from the room.

Anne knelt by her husband and joined in his weeping.

With her hands on her hips, Mary chastised her parents. "Why shed you tears? This is the child of God that I bear. We are to rejoice. Yahweh will protect us. Let us now lie down to rest. The sun will soon shine upon us and I must be on my way. My cousin Elizabeth has need of me."

Mary left them for her pallet and slept without dreaming.

Her parents remained in the courtyard. They talked through the night. They told each other their daughter knew not how hard the world could be to a divorced woman with child. They spoke of sending her away.

Though Joseph wished to be far from the house of Joachim, exhaustion overtook anger and he was forced to seek a place to rest. A half-moon provided light over the fields and he found an empty hut. He crawled inside, wrapped his mantle around his worn body and curled upon the dirt floor.

He had lived many years without a wife. Never had he felt this alone. Mourning overtook exhaustion. Joseph's pain was so great his bones ached. He beat his fist against the hard dirt floor and cried out. "Joachim how could you allow this? You made the marriage promise. It is your duty to protect your daughter until I take her into my house."

He wept and wondered how it was that his beautiful Mary could betray him? How had she fooled him? He had thought her the perfect woman. He rocked and tore at his clothes and hair. He cried out, "Jezebel, Jezebel! You have shamed yourself and your father and mother!"

Eventually he fell into a desperate sleep. In a dream he heard a strong voice coming from a silver cloud in a violet sky. "Joseph, put away your tears and anger. Your betrothed is blameless and pure as a newborn babe.

Mary is blessed among all women. God has chosen her to bear his Son, the Messiah for whom all have waited. You have been entrusted with the care of the Son of God until his time to be revealed. You and Mary will name him Emmanuel. Return to the house of Joachim. Take your wife to your house in Jerusalem. Care for and protect them. It is for this God has made you."

Joseph dreamed no more. A healing sleep overcame him until the sun rose high enough in the sky to send light into the hut. He woke refreshed and hungry. The dream remained vivid.

He rushed back to the house of Joachim to take Mary as wife.

CHAPTER EIGHT: A BLESSING ON BETHLEHEM

His First Year

Anne counted the weeks. Mary neared her time. She was too impatient to wait for a message from Joseph. She told Joachim, "I will walk if you do not give me Asia Two and the cart. You must not keep me here. My Mary has need of me."

Nothing Joachim said calmed Anne. He loaded the donkey cart for her and sent his youngest son Jacob with her. He promised Anne that he would arrange for her friend Naomi, the midwife, to follow.

Jacob and Anne traveled three days. In the evenings they found shelter in village squares. They shared the food Joachim had packed. They drew water for drinking and cleansing from village wells.

As they neared Jerusalem the road became congested with merchants and other travelers coming from and into the great city. Long lines of people, animals and wagons waited at the gates. Anne was relieved that they did not have to enter the city. She and Jacob had only to follow the lane that skirted the most northern wall to find her daughter.

The house of Joseph sat in a pretty spot near the Pool of Bethesda. It was a stone house the color of sand. Hay for Joseph's donkey lay stacked on the roof. Clay vessels flanking the doorway held oil and grains. A low wall covered with grape vines surrounded the courtyard. The gate was open.

Anne jumped from the cart and ran into the courtyard. She was astonished when she saw Mary standing next to a heavily laden donkey. Mary wore a dark brown tunic and matching mantle thrown over her head and shoulders.

"What is this?" Anne asked.

"Mother, how is that you are here? Has something happened to my father?"

"Why am I here? Why am I here? Do you think I cannot count? Look at the size of your belly. This is why I have come. Did you not think I would wish to be by your side?"

"Did Joseph send for you?"

"No. Joseph did not send for me. Must I ask permission to help birth my own grandson?"

Joseph came out of the house. "Mother Anne, may we give you water to drink? You look as if you have traveled far this day."

"Water. Water? You offer me water? What is this Joseph? How is it that I find my daughter appearing as if she were about to travel?"

"Mother Anne, have you not heard? A census is being taken. I am required to go to Bethlehem, the place of my birth. My family must be counted."

"Bethlehem?" Anne pointed to Mary. "You would take one such as she on such a journey?"

"Mother, mother. Calm yourself. I have chosen to go with Joseph. The Romans are more strict here than in Galilee. We must be counted. There is no need to worry. It is less than a day's walk.

Anne's face was scarlet. She shouted, "A long half-day's walk for one such as you. Daughter, have you lost your senses?"

Mary straightened. Her jaw set. "Mother, I am not ready to give birth. I can go with Joseph. I will go with my husband."

Leading Asia, Jacob entered the courtyard. He stopped the cart. He was too shocked to speak. Never had he seen the two women quarrel.

Mary remained calm. "Mother, I know that you have had a long walk. I wish that I had food and drink prepared for you, but I knew not that you were coming. There is grain and oil in the jars. The well is not far. Can you not stay in my husband's house? We will be gone not long."

With tears in her voice, Anne pleaded, "Daughter, this is dangerous. Do not take this action."

Joseph's donkey snorted and shifted his weight. Mary looked at the animal, then at her mother and husband. "Husband, we need not lock the house. My mother and Jacob will see to it that everything here remains safe."

Mary turned and walked out of the courtyard.

Joseph grabbed the rope looped around the neck of his donkey and followed Mary.

Anne dropped to her knees and wept.

Jacob ran after Mary and Joseph.

When Mary saw him she said, "Go back. Care for my mother."

It was the wife of the innkeeper who thought of the stable when she heard her husband turning away the couple who knocked late at the door despite no light coming from the inn. Drawn to the voices below, she hastily threw a mantel over her nightclothes and hurried down the stairs.

She thought it odd that light streamed through the open door. She was certain it was not morning. They had barely crawled upon their bedding when they heard the knock.

As soon as she saw the size of the belly of the woman before her, the innkeeper's wife knew the couple could travel no further. "Please forgive this suggestion," she said to Joseph. "We have no more rooms. I would not think of asking any woman in such a way as your wife to share a mattress with the mix of travelers who already lie in our rooms. There is an empty place in our stable. My husband cleaned it today and spread fresh straw upon the ground. You can rest there. You will be warm and safe."

Mary nodded to Joseph. Joseph helped her off the donkey.

The innkeeper and his wife led them to a crude stable with black goatskin roof and walls. At one end, a fence made from tree limbs penned a milking cow. At the other, a donkey was tied to a ring sewn into the rear wall. A goat slept on the floor inside the stable.

The innkeeper's wife said, "Husband, pull down from the roof a fresh bundle of hay. Spread it upon the floor and I will bring rugs and linen to cover."

Mary, who had told no one that she was in labor, groaned and held her stomach.

The older woman began giving orders to the men. "We must hurry. This woman is ready for birthing. Husband, send for the midwife."

Mary groaned again and bent over. She shook her head from side to side. "There is no time for a midwife," she whispered.

"Husband give over the hay to this man. He can spread it about." She turned to Joseph. "Sir, you must help me for I have no one else to call upon. Take your wife inside while I gather what is needed.

The innkeeper and his wife ran into the inn. She collected clean rags, a freshly laundered tunic, a small blanket, the gut of a lamb butchered that day, a sharp knife, a cake of salt and a short, strong stick no thicker than the finger of a woman. He pulled the linens from their bed.

In the stable Mary held her stomach and moaned as the frightened Joseph lowered her to the ground. Mary crouched on her hands and knees and rocked. Her hair fell around her face. The pains were quick and brutal.

After spreading the hay upon the ground, Joseph shook as he knelt beside Mary. Birthing was women's work. He knew nothing of it.

The innkeeper entered the stable. He placed the linens on the ground in a pile. His wife followed. She lined up the items she carried at the edge of the hay.

The innkeeper left and quickly returned with a large pitcher of water and two, large, shallow, clay bowls placing them near the hay. "Wife, I will be by the door." He left them.

The Innkeeper's wife went to Mary. "Dear one, I am Martha. I am here to help you. Come over to the pallet."

Mary cried out.

"Sir, you must assist your wife. Bring her here. Stand behind her and draw your arms beneath her arms."

Joseph lifted Mary and carried her to the place where Martha instructed. He supported her in the way the innkeeper's wife directed so that Mary squatted over the hay.

Martha put the stick between Mary's lips and placed a small blanket beneath her.

Mary moaned and bit hard on the stick as she suffered the agony of pushing out the babe. God was kind. The baby boy came quickly.

The woman pulled the blanket and the slippery baby from beneath Mary. She grabbed the left leg of the newborn, keeping it covered with a corner of the small blanket so that she would not lose her grip. She lifted the boy, feet skyward. She stuck the fingers of her free hand into his mouth and nose to clear his breathing passages.

The child wailed.

Mary, Joseph and Martha laughed in relief.

Martha handed the baby boy to Joseph and said, "With the gut of a lamb, tie the cord in two places and slice between them. After you rinse the blood from the child, crumble the salt and use it to rub clean his body. Take care to keep the salt away from his eyes! When your son is clean, rinse away the salt."

With a nod of her head, she gestured toward a stack of soft linens. "There are cloths to dry your son and cloths with which to wrap him." She turned back to Mary.

The nervous Joseph knelt on the ground. He placed the baby in a bowl and prayed, "Lord, guide my hands." He tied and cut the cord. With one hand he held the boy by the nape of his neck. With the other he poured water over him washing away blood mixed with birthing fluids.

The baby shuddered and cried.

Joseph placed him in the second bowl. The rough salt easily fell apart as Joseph worked it with one hand. He rubbed the crumbled salt on the skin of the newborn.

The baby cried louder.

Joseph rejoiced in the strength he heard in the wailing. He again poured water over the baby. He dried him and bound him with strips of pale cloth. He lifted the baby and held him close to his heart. He and the child were comforted.

Martha kneaded Mary's stomach to push out the afterbirth. This she placed into the basket. She helped Mary stand and removed her soiled tunic. She washed Mary, bound clean rags between her legs and dressed her in a clean, midnight blue colored tunic.

Mary touched Martha's face. "Thank you."

"Child, you have a beautiful son." She laughed and kissed Mary's face. "A healthy son, as all have heard."

Martha added the bloody tunic and cloths to the basket.

Joseph carried the baby to Mary.

The innkeeper called. "Is it over?"

"Yes, husband. Bring the broom."

The innkeeper came in and swept up the soiled hay and added it to the basket. He spread upon the floor fresh hay and over it spread the linens taken from his own bed. He picked up the bowls filled with bloody and salty water and followed his wife, who dragged the basket from the stable.

Together they made a fire in the stable yard and burned the afterbirth, the hay, the bloody cloths, Mary's soiled tunic, and the basket. When nothing but ashes remained, the woman swept them into a small, lidded crock.

The innkeeper poured the water and birthing fluids on the ground where the fire had burned. Lightning flashed from the spot. The stunned couple held each other, wondering the meaning of such a thing.

Inside the stable, Joseph helped Mary settle upon the linen covered hay. He knelt beside his wife and prayed. "Lord, I am not worthy to touch the soles of the feet of this child. I promise I shall protect him with my life."

Mary touched Joseph's face and saw that tears filled his eyes. "Husband, Yahweh is with us."

Joseph wrapped his mantle around Mary and Jesus and sat down behind her. He lifted his wife and the baby boy onto his lap. Cradling them in his arms, Joseph rejoiced in the health of the child and that his lovely Mary survived the birthing.

The pain of childbirth already a pale memory, Mary leaned against her husband and gazed at the perfect face of her son.

The boy opened his eyes.

Mary saw that his eyes were clear and that he studied her as she studied him. She held him close to suckle and joy filled her. She unwrapped his bindings and ran her hand over his small, faultless body. She counted each toe, each finger and cupped his tiny head in her hand to caress his fine golden hair. When the babe was satisfied, she wrapped him again in the soft cloth and watched him fall asleep.

It came to her that her bleeding had stopped and that her body had fully healed.

———————————

Using the manger for a cradle was the idea of the innkeeper. He cleaned the grain from a wooden trough and filled it with fresh, sweet smelling hay. He found a small, thin rug, softened long ago by his own babies. He placed it over the hay. He and his wife took the manger to the stable.

When the innkeeper placed the manger before her, Mary handed the baby to his wife.

Martha held him close and kissed his tiny head and felt the sweetness of holding a sleeping infant. She swayed with the babe cradled in her arms as she remembered when she first held her first child. A smile spread over her face. She was flooded with happiness. She felt loved. She grew weak and turned to her husband.

He took the child and watched his wife drop to her knees. "Wife, do you ail?"

"No, no, husband. I do not." She bowed her head.

The innkeeper pulled the baby close to his chest and felt a calm he had never before known. "Ah," he said, "this child, this child. Golden child. Golden child."

The old man knew not that he had spoken aloud. He carefully placed the baby boy in the manger he had lovingly prepared and knelt beside it. As had his wife, he bowed his head. "Lord God of Abraham, I know not the meaning of this night. I know only that we are blessed to be in the presence of this child. Lord God of Abraham, guide us."

The baby slept. Mary, Joseph, Martha and her husband sat in silence until from the road came the muted sounds of many voices.

The Innkeeper went out and saw a growing throng. Among them were citizens of Bethlehem who were awakened in their beds by the light streaming from the sky. Families brought by the census from faraway places left their tents and lined the road. Guests at the inn joined the crowd. The light drew shepherds from the hills, speaking of angels ordering them to follow the giant star that made the night so bright. Despite the cold and damp, all on the road waited calmly.

With Joseph's permission, the innkeeper rolled up the front wall of the stable. One by one the people came to Mary and Joseph and kneeled before the baby. Some who came left gifts. A woman pulled a coin from her veil and placed it on the ground. A man folded his finely woven mantle and handed it to Joseph. Children sang songs to the baby and left toys made of sticks.

Love from the child filled the air and wrapped around each who knelt there.

The crowd fell back when men dressed in rich fabrics and wearing elaborate headgear arrived on camels. They were amazed when these royal appearing persons bowed low to the babe in the manger and placed kingly gifts at the feet of Mary.

Mary, Joseph and the sweet baby spent the night before the quiet crowd.

Those who saw the baby felt his greatness. Some who came, but did not see him, believed the words of those who had. Others who did not see him doubted and left disappointed.

CHAPTER NINE: HEROD THE GREAT

His First Year

In Jerusalem, King Herod emerged from the dome atop a palace tower, onto the narrow ledge bordered by a waist-high wall.

"Leave," he ordered the soldier patrolling the parapet.

The sentry saluted Herod by throwing his right arm and fisted hand against his chest. He struck the stone floor three times with the blunt end of his spear, sending a message to the room below that he was leaving his post. As soon as Herod walked past him, he marched to the door and disappeared into the dome.

The tower was a place favored by Herod. Always he could find there a refreshing wind to carry from his body the stench of the whore in his bed.

He especially enjoyed being above the city in the dark of night when he could see winds pick up dying embers from fire pits and send them swirling above houses like fireflies dancing in a vast garden.

He needed no light to know that before him a wall built by his command connected his castle to the Temple. He needed no light to know that the Antonia Fortress built by his command butted the northern edge of the Temple. He needed no light to know soldiers by his command stood guard over the Temple grounds night and day, reminding all who knelt there that he is their king.

The light came from behind him, yet surrounded everything. Herod grumbled, "There is too much light this night. One can see a dog howling in an alley."

He turned and looked up. He could not admit to himself the terror he felt seeing the unusual star in the sky. He told himself that man rules the earth. The stars mean nothing to any but superstitious old women and weak old men. This was merely a dying star soon to burn out. It was nothing.

His thoughts turned to his visitors who claimed they were led by the star to a new king of the Jews. He was pleased how he handled them. He was certain his judicious questioning aroused in them no suspicions. He smiled at how he obtained their promise to return to him with word of where this new king could be found.

He laughed aloud, thinking of how they would carry disappointing news of having found no so such king. He would greet them as a father greets a lost son. He would dine with them and urge them to continue seeking. He would beg them send reports from the far ends of his kingdom until their quest was done. He shouted into the air, "Fools!"

The wind picked up and sent a chill through Herod. He was sick of the light of the star. He re-entered the dome and descended the stairs leading to his private chamber.

"Cover the windows," he ordered a waiting servant. "Is my bed empty?"

"Yes, sire."

"Are the linens clean?"

"Yes, sire."

"You are a good servant." He tore off his toga and threw himself naked upon the bed. "Get out," he ordered and closed his eyes.

CHAPTER TEN: IN THE BEGINNING

His First Year

It was not quite dawn, yet the room was lit as if the sun had fully risen. The innkeeper and his wife had worked all night, but neither was weary. They studied the room.

The floor was scrubbed. Fresh linens covered the straw-filled mattress. Beside it a clay pitcher holding fresh water sat in a bowl. A stack of clean cloths lay on the floor beside it.

"Wait," the man whispered to his wife and hurried from the room.

Martha dropped to her knees. She had lost count of the times she had said thanks to Yahweh since she heard the knock upon their door. New words would not come to her. *What,* she asked herself again, *had this night brought? How could it be that their tiny, poor inn could hold such a precious child?*

She had heard someone whisper, "He is divine." Many spoke of angels that night. She was almost certain she too had heard them sing.

The innkeeper returned with a smooth stone jar filled with fresh dirt from which grew blue flowers. "For the mother."

"This is good. Place them on the ledge of the window. The mother can look upon them while she rests."

The stable yard emptied by the time the sun rose and the great star blinked out. The older couple stood at the stable door. They begged permission to enter.

"Peace be with you," said the innkeeper.

"And also with you," answered Joseph as he pulled aside the goatskin wall.

"We bring you good news," said the old man. His wife finished his sentence. "We have prepared a room for you. You must use it, for you have had a full night. Mother and babe require rest."

Mary and Joseph accepted their generous offer.

As soon as they moved into the room, Mary and Jesus fell asleep on the mattress. Joseph slept on the floor wrapped in his cloak. The manger sat beneath the window.

For five days the holy family remained in Bethlehem. The days were spent waiting in long lines at tables set up near the village well. Scribes recorded family names and the count of people making up each family. On the fifth day Joseph's family was counted.

When the innkeeper learned the holy family would stay but one more night, he invited all who stayed at the inn to a special supper.

In a loud voice, the innkeeper instructed his wife to serve only the best wine. Mary laughed when she heard his wife sigh and mutter to the women as she poured, "As if I need be told. What does the man think? I would pour vinegar in your cups?"

The food was simple, the laughter ample. Happiness filled the little inn. The purity of Mary shone about her. It occurred to none that she be banished from their company.

Among them, there was an elderly man from Emmaus, and a man with a wife and three daughters from Yazith.

The old man from Emmaus with both hands held the baby high in the air, showing him to the guests reclining around the table. "Heavy is this one," he announced. "He could fill a bushel! He is strong. See how he holds his head."

A woman seated next to Mary whispered, "This is your first born? How is it you are able to sit at table?"

Another muttered to her husband, "Surely this is not a newborn babe? Look how clear his eyes."

The mother of the three girls asked that her daughters be allowed to hold the child. She guided each to hold him with care. In turn, each looked at the babe in wonder. "Mother, he smiled at me," claimed the eldest. "Me too, me too!" insisted the others.

"Ah, well, perhaps," she answered. The mother whispered to her husband, "Relief for the belly, I think." She took the baby from her child and immediately doubted her own words. He does smile. What child is this? She gave the boy back to Mary and spoke little for the rest of the evening.

As the sun rose on the sixth day, Joseph, Mary and the baby boy left the inn to return to Jerusalem. Those who had spent time with them wept at their departure.

The innkeeper buried the earthen crock containing the birth ashes at the place where the precious child was born. He marked the spot with the stone jug holding blue flowers.

CHAPTER ELEVEN: DOUBTING LABAN

Thirty-four Years After His Birth

When Anne again fell silent, Laban felt a terrible anxiety stir within. A chill ran through him as he remembered that the wide path from the house of Joses narrowed down to a faint trail cleverly hidden from the road. If this were the family of the crucified carpenter Jesus, they would be well served to hide.

Only the day before, as he accompanied his father to the village market, Laban had heard talk of a purge. Pilate was said to be sending out legions to hunt down and drag back in chains the followers of the man Jesus.

He pictured a man giving his father a bag of coins. Laban was certain his father would not send his only son into harm for any amount of money. His father could not have known Jesus of Nazareth was of this family.

The preacher lived in Nazareth. He worked as a carpenter and supported his widowed mother until he began to preach and lost his way. The house of Joses is only a half-day's walk from the village. Many from the village work these fields. If this were the family of the ill-fated carpenter, Laban reasoned, all in Nazareth would know of it. None here wear sackcloth and tear their hair. This is not a house in mourning. This cannot be the one of whom she speaks.

There are other reasons to hide the path to Joses' door. Thieves upon the road might think a profitable target the house of the owner of such bountiful fields. Romans march along this road. All who live along their path are wise to shutter their houses.

Is it not every woman's dream to be the mother of the Messiah? Mother Anne has given her daughter this honor. In her last years her poor mind dreams of angels and messages. Her family honors her. If the old woman wishes her dreams written, they allow it.

The latch clicked. Rebekah entered the garden carrying a bowl of broth, bread and a cup of water. Laban stood. His fears vanished.

"Mother Anne, the sun is high in the sky," Rebekah said. She placed the food and drink on the ground before Laban.

"Peace be with you," Laban managed.

"And also to you." Rebekah did not look at him when she answered.

Anne, roused by Rebekah's arrival, spoke to Laban. "You may remain here in the garden. I will return after a brief rest. Perhaps, in my absence, you will once again put ink to skin?"

Laban helped Anne to her feet and watched as Rebekah led her away and into the courtyard. He was surprised that fear could so quickly be replaced with delight. He laughed at himself and sat upon the ground and ate.

Laban looked at the skin spread out on the ground. He was not ready to put more words upon it. The story was too confusing. Perhaps he should find an opportunity to speak with his host to learn how thoroughly he should record this unlikely tale.

When he finished his meal, he rolled the skin and placed it in his sack. He laid the sack on the ground near Anne's chair. The shaded ground beneath the grapevines appealed to him. He settled there, leaning against the gate.

His mind returned to Mother Anne. Her body has outlived her mind, he decided. She speaks well, yet who could believe such a story? If there were any truth to it, every schoolboy would know it by heart. He relaxed. His full stomach and calmed nerves forced shut the lids of his eyes.

Laban was startled awake when from the courtyard he heard the singing of women. He turned his ear to the gate, for this was a prayer unknown to him.

Our father in heaven, we honor your name.
Your kingdom has come to earth.
We live as if in heaven.
You give us each day food and drink.
You protect us from evil.
Forgive us our sins as we forgive those who sin against us. Amen.

The singing ended. Laban heard the soft chatter of women and the laughter of children. He heard the roll of the millstone and the rhythmic slap of a shuttle flying across the loom. He knew that the afternoon rest was past. He moved away from the gate to a place near Mother's Anne chair.

He stood, puzzling over the prayer he had heard. It was brief. It contained a difficult commandment. Forgive us if we forgive? Why would they ask such a thing? Only God can forgive sin. Whom might he forgive? He had no enemy.

For what should he be forgiven? He thought of the lovely Rebekah and the sway of her hips as she walked away from him. This is not a sin, he told himself. This is not something for which I need be forgiven. He could not repress his smile when the gate opened and he saw that it was Rebekah who entered.

"Peace be with you." She looked into his eyes as she spoke.

"And also with you," his smile broadened.

"Mother Anne has found storytelling more demanding than she expected. She asks that you forgive her for not returning to the garden. She says she will again speak with you when the sun rises above the hills. My mother has sent me to ask if you have need of food or drink."

"The hospitality of the house of Joses in generous. I do thirst."

"Come and I will draw water for you." Rebekah turned away from him.

Laban picked his sack from the ground and followed her into the courtyard. He hardly noticed the women working and the children playing there. Nor did he note that the women grew silent and hushed the children as he and Rebekah entered.

Laban lowered his bag of writing tools onto the ground next to the well. He grabbed the rope before Rebekah could reach for it and drew up a leather bucket filled with cold water.

From the lip of the well Rebekah picked up a cup carved from a gourd. She hoped Laban would not notice the slight tremor of her hands as she held it out to him.

Laban filled the gourd from the leather bucket. He let loose the ropes allowing the bucket to fall hard into the water. He accepted the gourd offered by Rebekah.

As he drank the water, he also drank in the beauty of her face. Dark brows curved above almond-shaped eyes, shaded by thick black lashes. Her complexion was fairer than most. Her lips seemed to smile, whether she ordered so or not. Her hair fell around her face like a beautifully woven mantel. Laban longed to touch her.

Rebekah flushed in Laban's intense study. Rather than looking down or turning away, she glanced beyond him. When she spoke, her voice seemed guarded. "You may store your goods here. They will be safe in the courtyard. You are free to walk about the hill, or rest as you wish. I regret that tasks await me. Please forgive me for leaving you without company."

Rebekah caught a glimpse of disappointment in the eyes of the scholar as she turned away from him. Thrilled, but realizing she was being carefully observed, she did not allow the smile in her heart to show upon her face.

"Peace be with you."

Laban had heard no one approach. He jumped and spun around at the sound of a deep voice behind him. He saw a smiling man dressed for fieldwork. His rough, sleeveless tunic was tucked into his girdle. He wore no mantle.

Laban judged the man to be only a few years his elder. "Peace be with you," he answered.

The women working in the courtyard sang out greetings to the new arrival. He smiled and waved his hands, speaking only to Laban. "I am Daniel, son of Joses. My father sends me from the fields to greet you. It grieves him that this he cannot do. We are harvesting the wheat and he is needed among the rows as long as the sun stays above the hills. He begs your forgiveness."

Laban paused. Twice now I am asked to forgive. Is what the prayer meant so simple? Aloud he said, "I am the servant of you and your father."

"Welcome brother to the house of Joses. Have you eaten?"

"I have been well cared for. I have had food and drink. Already this day the widow of Joachim has shared her words with me."

"Do I interrupt your work?"

"No. I have been told we will meet when the sun next appears above the hills." Feeling a need to explain why he was standing amid the women and children, he added and nodded towards the sack on the ground, "I was about to put away the skin and ink."

Daniel scooped up the sack. "Please allow me to do so for you. My father insists that you stay in the upper room, for you honor our family by traveling from Nazareth to record the words of Mother Anne. I shall place your belongings there. They will be near at hand when you have need of them." In two broad steps Daniel was at the steps and moving upward.

The shocked Laban stood unmoving. To stay in an enclosed upper room was a privilege never before bestowed upon him. The gesture of respect humbled Laban. He was swept by a wave of gratitude for the insistence of his mother that he be diligent with his studies. He had barely completed this thought when Daniel returned.

"Please follow." Daniel led the scholar past the garden gate and through the garden to an upward path. He stopped a short distance from the top of the hill. They stood on a rock outcropping and looked over a grey canopy of olive tree branches.

Below and to his left, Laban saw patches of stubble where the harvested barley fields lay waiting for clearing and replanting. To his right he saw lines of men slicing wheat stalks, the sharpened, curved blades of their scythes flashing in sunlight. Women and boys followed, bundling the grains. In the distance, he saw the dark green circle of a threshing field, a cluster of huts nearby.

Opposite the wheat fields, Laban saw that a row of tall cypress trees shielded a slanted pasture from the sight of travelers along the road. There a pair of oxen and two donkeys grazed amid blue and white flowers.

Daniel spoke. "I regret our hospitality is not as it should be. All able are needed to harvest the wheat. I must return to work as long as the sun will allow."

Even Laban, a child of the village, knew the harvest was abundant. "I have been relieved of my duty here for the day. If you show me what to do, might I be of help?"

Daniel repressed a smile, thinking of what his father would say if he found the soft hands of the scholar blistered by the scythe. "It is a generous offer. The house of Joses is a house of women," he laughed. "My father and I are the only able bodied men, but we do not ask our guests to work our fields. We return from the fields when the sun sets. My father looks forward to an evening in your company. He will be glad of news from Nazareth. We ask that you forgive us for leaving you."

Laban marveled at being again asked to forgive. Forgive, a word frequently used. A practice he had not before noted. Laban looked about. He saw that the path continued upward. "May I have your permission to follow the path?"

"Feel free to walk where you wish. The path will always return you to the clearing and my father's house."

"Thank you."

"Peace be with you."

"And also with you," answered Laban as he watched Daniel walk to the side of the rock outcropping and work his way down the steep slope to the edge of the olive grove.

Daniel waved and disappeared into the stand of trees.

Laban was buoyed by this unexpected freedom. He followed the path upward. At the broad, treeless hilltop he stood amid purple and yellow wildflowers growing around and between exposed reddish-brown boulders.

Behind him, hills to the east hid the village of Nazareth.

He glimpsed winding pieces of the road he had traveled to find the house of Joses. To the north he could see perched upon a high mesa the glistening white walls of Sepphoris.

At his feet, he saw that the path on which he stood crossed the hill and began to slope downward. He decided to follow it. He discovered a ledge from which water splashed into a small pool. From the pool, a narrow stream curved downward. He followed the stream to a place above the line of olive trees where it vanished into a larger pool.

Laban considered bathing. He was about to remove his mantle and tunic when he heard voices of women. Feeling as if he were an intruder Laban dropped to the ground using for cover the high reeds and grasses at the pool's edge.

Three women came out of the olive grove. Their conversation easily carried across the water.

Laban recognized the voices of Rebekah and Sarah. The third was unknown to him. He wished he had made his presence known, rather than dropping to the ground. They will think he had come to spy on them as they beat their laundry against the rocks. He feared he would bring shame upon his father's house. He dared not move and could not see that the women brought no laundry to the pool. Laban closed his eyes and prayed they could not hear the sound of his breath. When he heard Sarah issue an order, his prayer became urgent.

"Ruth, remove your clothing and immerse yourself. Now that you are a woman each month your body will empty itself of impurities. When your days of bleeding have ceased you will come here for cleansing. Give Rebekah your soiled tunic. I have a fresh garment for you."

"Do it quickly," Rebekah advised. "You need only to go in up to your neck. Then you may consider yourself clean."

Ruth disrobed and yelped when she entered the cold water.

Laban pushed his face into the ground. He did not wish to spy upon this private ritual. He was terrified. How, he wondered, could he explain hiding in the grasses?

He heard the water splash. He heard Sarah order Ruth from the water. He heard Rebekah laugh as she tossed a drying cloth to Ruth.

He heard Ruth ask, "Must we do this in the midst of winter?"

Rebekah answered. "Yes, we must. Believe me you will know then that today the water is warm!"

"It is a small sacrifice. For without the period of impurity we would be unable to bear children, the Lord God of Abraham's greatest gift to women," Sarah reminded Rebekah.

"Is the water too cold for bathing?" Rebekah asked Ruth.

Sarah chastised her daughter, "It is not for pleasure we are here."

Laban tried not to think of Rebekah bathing in the water, but images overpowered him. He imagined her bare arms creating gentle waves. He saw her dark hair floating on the water, spreading out around her sweet face. He pictured her exposed skin glistening in summer sunshine. He buried his face deeper into the reeds.

The women left the pool unaware of the presence of Laban. They walked the same broad path that had brought them up from the courtyard. Sarah, who seemed always to rush, quickly outpaced the younger women.

When Rebekah was certain Sarah was too far ahead to hear her speak, she whispered, "The scholar Laban arrived today."

"Rebekah, your face grows as scarlet as the cloak of a Roman soldier," cried the astonished Ruth.

"Quiet," Rebekah admonished. "It is not so," she snapped and quickened her steps, her face growing redder.

Amused, Ruth kept pace with Rebekah. "This scholar is handsome, is this not so?"

Rebekah marched forward ignoring Ruth. She wished that she had not spoken. Were her feelings embroidered upon the sleeves of her tunic?

Ruth stopped. She sounded injured. "Cousin, why do you run from me?"

Rebekah relented. She turned back to Ruth. She held her finger to her lips. "Be quiet," she mouthed and whispered, "Yes, he is handsome. He has dark curls and a broad smile. He looks strong and able."

"You are fond of this scholar. I can hear it in your voice. You smile as you speak of him." She was thoughtful. "What are you to do?"

"Do? Am I to do something?"

"Yes. I think you must. I see that he has affected you. You must tell your mother. You do not know but that she and your father have already found a husband for you. You must tell them you have feelings for the scholar. Laban is his name?"

"Yes, Laban." Rebekah's voice softened when she said his name. She became sad. "I cannot speak of this to any. He is the son of the potter in Nazareth. They are not of our ways."

"Speak to Mother Anne. She is not as strict as our mothers. If I met a man who made my eyes sparkle and my cheeks redden at the sound of his name, I would run to her and beg her to speak for me."

"You sound as if you have thought much on this. Have you met such a man?"

"No. Though I have dreamed of such a man. Have not you?"

"I have wondered what man might be chosen for me. To choose for myself? This is not possible."

Ruth looked down at her feet and closed her eyes. Tears pushed against her eyelids. "I know I sound foolish. Yet, I swear to the Lord God of Abraham, I have heard of such. Some women are allowed to choose."

"You sound strong, not foolish. I beg you, speak not to any of what you have wrung from me this day. The scholar may be gone before the Sabbath comes. Once his work here is done we may never see him again. I do not wish to disgrace the house of Joses with my silly thoughts. You must swear to silence."

"I will keep your secret. I know that it is not for us to decide whom to marry. Yet, I see some wives welcome husbands home from the fields more eagerly than do others. If God blesses her, a woman knows love after she is betrothed. We are taught that love of others matters more than all else. Why can we not dream of a special love in marriage?"

Rebekah had no answer.

Ruth sought to comfort Rebekah. "Though we may not choose, no woman in this house is forced to marry a man she does not wish."

"Ruth, this man will not be chosen for me. It matters not whom they choose."

The saddened young women walked in silence until they came level with the clearing. They heard Sarah calling and hurried their steps, speaking no more of Laban.

Laban was grateful the women did not tarry at the pool. He lay frozen in place until he felt certain they were safely away.

He rose and washed his face. He worked his way up, over and down the hill. In Anne's garden, he heard the sounds of women working in the courtyard. He smelled the ever-present scent of food upon the courtyard fire.

Laban sat upon the ground and prayed. "Lord God of Abraham, you know that I had no wrong in my heart when I hid in the rushes. If any person saw me lying there, I beg you remove such a memory from his mind." In a few moments he slept.

When the sun dipped behind the hill, Daniel came for him. "My father waits."

Laban quickly came awake and jumped up. He followed Daniel through the garden gate. He saw Joses standing in the courtyard near a square of rugs.

Joses was not a tall man, but he stood in a way that made him seem larger than those around him. His waist was thick. Silver strands ran through his long brown hair and beard. As did Daniel, Joses appeared freshly washed and wearing clean robes.

Joses embraced Laban and kissed the sides of his face. "Peace be with you and welcome to my house. I am Joses, son of Jude, the second born son of Joachim."

"Peace also to you. I am honored to be present in the house of Joses. The hospitality of this house if far greater than I deserve," Laban honestly replied.

"Sit with me when we eat, which I trust will be soon. I know my stomach says so," he laughed. "I wish to hear news from Nazareth." Joses turned, looking for his wife. "Sarah, bring water to our scholar, so that he may wash."

Laban washed and dried his feet and hands and the three men sat upon the rugs. He felt his heart soar when he saw that it was Rebekah who carried saucers of oil to lamp stands near the rugs. "Peace be with you," he greeted as he watched her light the wicks of the lamps.

"And also with you," she answered and went about her work.

A woman not much younger than Rebekah approached grasping the hands of two small boys.

"Ah," said Joses, "the little ones come." When they reached the rugs, Joses rose and the woman released them. He presented them to Laban, "This is the first-born son of my brother James. His name is Ezral. He is named for my long dead cousin Ezral, the first-born son of my uncle David, the first-born son of Joachim."

Laban squatted on the rug so that his face was at the level of Ezral. "Peace be with you, Ezral."

The child smiled. "Peace also to you," he answered and allowed Laban to kiss his cheeks.

With his knee, Joses nudged the second boy to Laban's side. "This is Eyal, second son of James. Named for my long dead cousin Eyal, second son of David."

Laban turned to him. "Peace be with you."

"Peace be to you," the child whispered and buried his head in the folds of Joses robes.

Joses laughed. "Forgive the boy, Laban. He is hardly weaned from his mother's breast."

Laban stood and joined Joses' laughter. "They are strong, healthy boys. Your house is blessed."

"We are blessed!" Joses nodded toward Daniel. "Without these two,

Daniel and I are far outnumbered! This is their sister Ruth, daughter of James." Joses said turning toward the woman who brought the children to the rug.

"Peace be with you," she said with a slight bow of her head.

Laban's heart stilled. This was the voice of the third woman at the pool. Does she know that I hid in the reeds? He found voice, "Peace be with you," he answered, returning the hint of a bow.

"Sit, sit Laban," ordered Joses. "The women bring food."

The men sat facing the fire. Joses took the shy Eyal into his lap. Ezral sat between Daniel and Laban.

Sarah carried to them a large clay bowl, containing a thick barley broth flavored with bits of carrots and onion. This she placed in the center of the rug. "Husband, the food is warm. Do not delay the prayer," she admonished.

Deborah, wife of James, followed carrying a pitcher of wine. Daniel and Joses held up wooden cups they found at the edge of the rug. Laban did likewise. Saying nothing, Deborah filled their cups.

Joses whispered to Laban, "It is good being in a house full of women. We are well cared for," He laughed. Then he rose from the rug. Laban, Daniel and the young boys also stood. The women ceased their labors and turned toward Joses.

Joses raised his cup into the air. "Lord God of Abraham, we thank you for the blessings you bring upon this house. We thank you for the presence of our scholar, Laban. May you bless his labor in this house. Amen."

Sarah carried a basket of round breads to Joses. He took bread and passed the basket to Daniel.

Laban saw the women and girl children arrange themselves along a long row of rugs. He did not see Mother Anne among them. Did she ail? He was surprised to discover such a thought saddened him. Already, the old woman had touched his heart.

He watched Rebekah and Ruth serve the women and girl children. Ruth handed each a round of flatbread. Rebekah brought to them a bowl from which each, using their bread, scooped a portion of barley soup into a small cup.

Joses took his bread and dipped it into the large bowl set upon the square rug. "Eat, Laban," he said motioning that Laban too should dip his bread into the bowl.

The meal was quick and noisy for as soon as Joses took his first bite the women began to chatter.

Joses ate, fed Eyal and asked, "So Laban, what news bring you from Nazareth?"

Laban chewed the bread in his mouth and swallowed. He wiped his mouth with his sleeve. "We have been most blessed. In the length of only one cycle of the moon we have added three sons to our village."

"God has been generous. Which of my friends has God so blessed?"

"Amos the baker was the first. Before the next Sabbath Tobias the sandal maker raised a boy child to the skies."

"Tobias, you say?" Joses turned to Daniel, laughter in his voice. "He must be thanking the Lord daily, he has waited long for a son to join his household."

The remark did not surprise Laban. Tobias' wife had given him six daughters. The whole village had been surprised and delighted by the birth of a boy to this house. "The son of Mahlon was also blessed."

"Micha? He was but a child hiding behind his mother's skirts the last I saw him. Grown with a family of his own?"

"He has taken the house of his father. I am sorry to bear this news. The bones of Mahlon are at rest. He fell from a parapet. Thanks be to God, he did not suffer long."

"Mahlon was a good man. It grieves me to learn this news." Joses sighed. "There must be other news. Is this not so?"

"Yes. The ditches we dug before the winter rains worked. This year the paths before our houses remained hard and easy to use. It was a blessing to us all. For many months now the Romans pass by us."

"This is always good news."

Laban decided not to share the fears he had heard expressed in the market. Word travels along the road. Joses would learn soon enough. The house of Joses was well protected. "It is quiet in the village with many laboring in the fields. I am afraid this is all I have of which to speak."

"My wife tells me we have put you to work this day."

"Sir, it is not work to listen to the words of Mother Anne." Afraid he may have offended, he quickly added, "The widow of Joachim has asked that I speak of her as Mother, else I should not be so bold."

Joses laughed. "As do we all. Worry not, when you are in this house you are one of us."

"The generosity of this house cannot be surpassed. Sir, I see that Mother Anne does not share this meal. I hope she does not ail."

"No, no, Laban. Mother Anne has already taken bread. She finds her pallet early." He leaned in to Laban. "She also leaves her pallet early. She will have your ears ringing before the sun clears the hills."

"Her stories are intriguing and complex. I would be grateful of your guidance as to which of that she speaks I should set in ink."

Joses grew thoughtful. He wished James had not asked this of Mother Anne. Jesus is with us always, but Mary, who was lost to her and restored, is lost to her once more. He thought of his brothers James and John who, like Mary, walked the earth sharing The Word. They knew not the burdens they left behind. Joses sighed. Perhaps reliving the days our dear Jesus lived here consoles Mother Anne. "Laban, what has Mother Anne asked of you?"

The scholar considered the promise he had made. "To record with integrity all that she says," he answered.

"So be it."

Joses rose and all, including Laban, followed. Joses prayed, "Lord God of Abraham, we thank you for the food you give us each day. We thank you for the many blessing you have brought to this house. Amen."

Children were collected and taken into the hill. Cups and bowls were carried away and washed. One by one the women disappeared into the hill leaving one lamp lit for Joses, Daniel and Laban.

"Laban, on another night we shall sit near the fire to speak of many things. Our harvest days are long and my pallet calls. Please have no offense. Forgive me for leaving you to Daniel."

Laban nearly laughed. Again asked to forgive? "Worry not. There is nothing to forgive. Thank you for making me welcome in your house."

"Here, Daniel. Take the lamp. Lead our scholar to his bed."

"Yes, father." Daniel kissed his father.

Joses turned to Laban, embraced him and kissed his face. "You are as one of my own," he told him.

Laban believed him.

Joses turned away and left them for his room in the hill.

Daniel stood with the oil lamp in his hand.

Laban saw that Daniel appeared weary. "I am certain your pallet sings out as well, for you have had a full day. I thank you for leaving your work to welcome me."

"Come, Laban." Daniel went to the steps curving up the wall to the upper room.

Laban followed. He was not surprised to share a room with Daniel. The house of Joses would not insult a guest by leaving him alone in the night.

Daniel placed the lamp upon an overturned basket. Its flame cast long shadows upon the walls. Two sleeping rugs had been spread upon the hard-packed dirt floor. The window was open. Daniel flopped on a rug and pulled it around him. He was asleep in seconds.

Laban sat upon the second rug. He was not ready for sleep. His head buzzed from the surprises brought by the day: the surprise of finding the house of Joses hidden from the road; the surprise of meeting the beautiful Rebekah; the surprise of being treated with the respect extended a man. It pleased him to think he was no longer the boy who only that morning had left his father's house.

He moved the oil lamp to the floor and next to it he spread the hairless goatskin upon which he had written the words: "The Book of Anne." He sat for a long time, thinking of all that Anne had told him. Fully framing each sentence in his mind, he wet the brush and began writing her story.

Angels appeared to the Nazarene farmer Joachim foretelling of a birthing by his wife, saying it would be a girl child who would be blessed among all women. There was much celebration in the house of Joachim. When she was born they named her Mary.

The child grew to woman and was betrothed to Joseph of the house of David. While still in the house of Joachim, the angel Gabriel appeared to Mary saying she carried in her womb the child of God – a boy child whom she would name Emmanuel.

In a dream, a voice coming from a cloud told Joseph, her betrothed, to take her as wife so that no earthly dishonor would come to the child of God. Angels sang at the child's birth in the town of Bethlehem. Many pilgrims bearing gifts came to see him and to proclaim him the Messiah.

When he finished writing, Laban reread what he had written. He decided it mattered not that he believed what he wrote. He had kept his promise to Mother Anne.

Laban fell asleep and dreamed of Rebekah. He woke to the aroma of bread baking. The sun had not yet risen. For a moment he thought he breathed his mother's cooking.

Faint light began to creep into the sky and through the open window. Laban remembered his dreams of Rebekah as he came awake. He saw that Daniel had rolled his rug and left it leaning against a wall. He rose, rolled his rug, and carefully placed it next to the rug left by Daniel.

Laban saw the skin upon the floor. After ensuring that the ink had dried, he rolled the skin and placed it in his bag. He descended the steps thinking of angels.

Daniel stood in the courtyard near his father. Sarah worked at the fire pit. Laban was disappointed that he did not see Rebekah there.

Joses greet Laban with enthusiasm. "Wash your ears well today. Mother Anne is certain to fill them!" Joses laughed.

The ritual of breaking fast began. The women carried water and cloths to the men for washing. They replaced the water bowls with bowls of broth. Joses prayed, "Blessed are you Lord who causes bread to come from the earth. Amen."

When the bowls were wiped clean and the bread swallowed, Joses again stood to pray. "When you have eaten and are full, then you shall bless the Lord your God for the good land which he has given you."

Daniel and Laban added their own "Amens." Daniel and Joses left for the fields.

Sarah collected the bowls, acknowledging the presence of Laban with a nod.

Laban decided to go to the garden to await Anne.

"Peace be with you, Laban."

It was Rebekah's sweet voice. Laban turned to see her lovely face. He felt a smile upon his lips. "And also with you," he responded. He wished to say more, but he found himself mute. It was all that he could do to look at her without reaching out to touch her.

Rebekah returned his smile. "Mother Anne will always speak with you in the garden. It is the one place she finds comfortable. It is there you should wait. Can you find your way?"

He nodded. Did she think him dim-witted? He had only to pass through the gate to find the garden. He found voice and was surprised by his question. "Will you be with us today?"

"I have many duties. I help with the children of the house. Perhaps when they nap, I can come to hear Mother Anne's stories." Rebekah wished to linger in the presence of Laban. She asked, "Did you rest well?"

"I did. Many thanks to the hospitality of this house."

"This house is blessed by your presence." Rebekah felt bold. Laban seemed shy in her company. She knew not why this pleased her.

Seeing the two standing close, Sarah called out, "Rebekah, have you no tasks?"

"Yes, mother," she answered. To Laban she said, "I must go. Peace." She left, vanishing behind a latticed door before he could manage a reply.

Laban hurried to the gate nearly hidden behind the fig tree. He was surprised to find Anne sitting in her chair, a well-worn, finely woven cloth the color of peaches wrapped around her shoulders. "Mother Anne, forgive me. I knew not that you awaited."

"Pay it no mind, Laban. I often wake well before the sun. My old bones protest, yet my mind insists that I rise. Have you been well fed?"

"Yes, Mother Anne. I am well cared for."

"That is as it should be. Make yourself comfortable, for I have much to say."

As he had the day before, Laban settled at the feet of Anne.

Anne began without preamble. "I behaved badly at the house of Joseph. I was frightened for my Mary. She was heavy with child. I was certain she was walking into a terrible danger. I become distraught. Yet, even then, I could not imagine the sorrows that awaited."

CHAPTER TWELVE: ANGER AND JOY

His First Year

Having no knowledge of the safe birth in Bethlehem, Anne's fears grew each day of Mary and Joseph's absence. She was certain thieves had beset them on the road. Perhaps Mary had begun birthing somewhere desolate between Jerusalem and Bethlehem? She imagined both mother and child lying wrapped in burial clothes with a grief-maddened Joseph tearing at his hair and garments.

Each day she swore at the Romans. That they should force such a trip filled her with hatred. Her anger with Joseph grew. May the Lord God of Abraham forgive her, she was also angry with Mary.

Anne shuttered the windows of the house of Joseph. She threw herself against the walls. She pulled at her hair.

Locked out, Jacob was unable to console her. He went into the city and hired a fast horse. He raced to the house of Joachim. He told his father of Mary's condition and that she and Joseph journeyed to Bethlehem. He told Joachim of Anne's madness.

Joachim exchanged places with Jacob and forced the horse to return to Jerusalem the same day his son brought news of his wife's illness.

When he arrived at the house of Joseph he left the sweating animal in the courtyard and beat down the door. He found his wife sitting in the loft, weeping. He gathered her into his arms, "Anne, Anne – you must not continue this mourning. You know not that they have come to harm. God would not have placed Mary in Joseph's hands if he could not keep her safe."

Anne was filled with shame for the smallness of her faith.

"Husband, forgive me. I have caused you much concern and time away from the fields."

"Worry not, wife." He helped her stand and led her into the courtyard. "Wife, let me wash you. Where do I find water and clean garments?"

"Husband, it is enough that you are here. I have regained my senses." She looked about her. "Please, go into the city to return the horse. While you are gone, I shall clean myself and prepare the house for our daughter's return."

Joachim studied his wife. She stood straight. Her tears had dried. Her eyes were clear. When she asked if Naomi, the midwife, followed him to Jerusalem, he knew that her mind had healed. "I have sent Jude for her. She will not be long in coming."

"This is good."

"Wife?"

"Yes, Joachim."

"Where is the well? I cannot return the horse to his owner until I have tended to him. He needs water and grain."

"The well is but a few steps along the lane. Husband, Joseph keeps large vessels of water lined along the back of his house. It is there he tends his donkey."

Joachim fed and gave the horse drink. He washed the animal, brushed his coat, cleaned his hoofs and combed his mane and tail.

By the time Joachim left for the city, Anne had cleansed herself and was scrubbing the floors and walls of the house of Joseph.

Anne was throwing cloths to dry over thorn bushes growing outside the courtyard wall when she heard a donkey bray. She looked up from her work and saw that they came.

Her scarf fell, her hair streamed out behind her head and the hem of her tunic flapped above her knees as she ran to them. "My child, my child! It is you!" Anne rejoiced.

When she reached the donkey, she laid her head on its neck and bawled. "I thank the Lord God of Abraham, it is you!"

Mary smiled and leaned across the animal. She held out to her mother a small bundle.

Anne was certain her heart would fly from her chest when she took the child into her arms. Later she would swear by the Lord God of Abraham that in that very moment the child loved her.

Joseph spoke. "Greetings, Mother. Peace be with you."

"Ah, Joseph. So, were you counted?" It was not a kind welcome and later Anne was sorry that she had said it. She turned to Mary, "My daughter, are you well? I have been frightened for you."

"I am well, Mother."

Mary's answer meant nothing to Anne. She would not rest until the midwife examined her daughter.

Joseph helped Mary down from the donkey so that she might walk beside her mother. As they passed houses along the lane, gates opened and greetings of peace and welcome were called out to them.

Anne insisted on lifting Jesus high, so that all they passed could see him. Some friends came into the street. All complimented Mary and Joseph on how robust was the child.

Mary's neighbor Rachael came to greet them. On her hip she carried her own baby boy. A daughter barely able to walk gripped the skirt of her tunic.

Anne proudly showed Rachael her grandson.

"A son, you say? He favors Mary. This is a blessing. It is a good omen when the first-born son resembles his mother." Rachael asked Joseph, "Have you chosen a name?"

Mary answered. "His name will be Emmanuel."

"Emmanuel?"

"Yes." Mary smiled. "This is the name chosen for him."

Rachael's face revealed her shock. Though Joseph was known as a skilled and busy carpenter, the couple lived quietly in their small Jewish enclave. She often chatted with Mary at the well. Never would she have guessed Mary and Joseph would be so arrogant as to give a son such a name.

Mary took Rachael's son from the woman's arms and instructed Anne to give her own infant son to the woman.

Rachael took the baby and looked into his dark, clear eyes. She was enthralled and troubled. She quickly returned him to his grandmother. To Mary she said, "This is a beautiful, healthy baby. You are blessed."

Mary gave Rachel's own baby boy back to her. "Peace be with you."

"And also with you," Rachael replied as she closed her gate. In troubled silence, she watched Mary and her family walk away. When she had held the child, she had felt strength wrapped in softness. Her mind told her that such a thing was a blessing, yet her heart was disturbed.

In moments, Mary and Anne, who carried the baby, returned to the house of Joseph. As Joseph tended his donkey, Anne helped her daughter resettle into the small, neatly tended house.

Joachim, having accomplished his mission to return the horse to its owner, was thrilled to see his Mary when he entered Joseph's courtyard.

"Papa, Papa!" Mary cried out when he came through the gate. She ran to her father.

Relieved and delighted to see his daughter, Joachim embraced her and kissed her face. "My beautiful child, are you well?" Before Mary could answer, he saw Anne coming from the house with the child in her arms. "It is true, then? We have a boy child?"

"Yes, Papa, it is so."

Anne brought the child to Joachim.

He took the babe in his arms. Joachim had held newborn sons and grandsons. He loved all of them. With this one, he felt loved. Savoring the feeling, he held the child close to his heart. When he remembered his daughter, he asked again, "Mary, are you well?"

"Yes, Papa, I am. Though I confess the trip has made me weary. I long to lie upon my pallet."

Joachim gave the baby to his daughter. "My child, go and rest. Your mother yearns to care for you. Pay me no mind. Rest."

"Yes, Mary," added Joseph. "Go find your pallet. Mother Anne and I can take care of Joachim.

Mary smiled at her husband. "Thank you." To her father, she said, "Thank you for being here. Tomorrow we shall take the baby to the Temple to be named. She carried the child into the house and lay upon the linens in the loft and took the babe to breast. Soon both slept.

Anne worked at the fire. She stirred cold ashes. She threw upon them small bundles of dried grass. She took a piece of flint and struck it against the bottom of an iron pot. A spark ignited the grass. Anne added more grass until the coals began to glow.

A neighbor arrived with a crock of seasoned lamb stew with bits of carrot and garlic. Another brought freshly baked loaves of bread, olive oil and spices. Another brought radishes and cooked fava beans. All were invited to return the next day to celebrate the naming of the baby.

Calm settled upon the house of Joseph. Anne served the men and took food into the house to share with Mary. When the sun left the sky, Joachim and Joseph slept rolled in rugs atop the roof. Anne shared the pallet in the loft with Mary. Before they slept, Mary whispered to her mother the story of all that had occurred in Bethlehem.

All but Anne slept well that night. Peace would not come to her mind. She rolled from side to side thinking of all that Mary had told her. *Mary healed? This is not possible. Why had not Joachim brought Naomi with him?* The waiting was terrible for her.

As the sun began to spread light into the sky, Anne rose from the bed. She left the sleeping Mary and baby to tend the fire.

As she worked, Anne tried to think through her conflicting feelings. She was grateful Mary had received good care in Bethlehem. Yet she harbored anger toward Joseph, for he robbed her of a moment between a daughter and mother that framed a bond no man could understand.

She stirred the barley grain into flatbread dough and was careful not to speak aloud her thoughts, as she might otherwise do when working alone. She chastised herself. *It is not right to hold hard feelings against any person. Certainly, it is of no good to do so against the husband of a daughter. I must put aside this anger. It is done. From now forward all is about the child.*

Anne threw the bread dough onto the bottom of a large iron roasting pan. It cooked quickly. She turned it with a flat stick so that it would not burn.

The aroma of fresh bread woke the men. Joseph was the first to climb down the ladder leaning against the side of the house. "Peace, mother. Have you all that you need?"

No, I do not. Had Mary been here with me, I would have known to send a boy to ask my husband to bring eggs for the celebration. And meal and honey for cakes! Aloud, she said, "I do, Joseph. Your house is in good order. I find it easy to work here."

"This is as it should be. Have you need of fresh water? Shall I go to the well?"

Joachim climbed down the ladder. "Ah, wife, it is good to smell your bread upon the fire." He smiled at Anne, happy to see her behaving as he expected. He knew nothing made Anne happier than taking care of Mary.

"Husband, did you sleep well?"

"I did. I slept so soundly I did not hear the baby cry."

"You did not hear the baby cry, husband, because the baby does not cry."

At that moment they heard wailing from the loft. The three laughed.

Again Joseph asked, "Mother, have you need of fresh water?"

"Thank you, Joseph. The water jug can wait until the two of you have broken your fast." Pointing as she spoke, she directed Joachim. "Husband, there are rugs lying just inside the doorway."

Joachim retrieved the rugs and spread them on the ground. The men stood upon them. They prayed. They sat and allowed Anne to serve them flatbreads and cups of reheated stew. When they finished eating they stood again and prayed thanks to the Lord God of Abraham.

Joseph turned to Joachim. "I go now to the well. Come with me, so that the women there do not laugh in their veils at the sight of a man doing their work. Two men doing the work of one woman honor them and they will not think me a fool."

Anne ignored Joseph's jest. She said nothing when he and Joachim left the courtyard with Joseph carrying a clay pot upon his shoulder. Before they were out of the yard, Anne carried to Mary a bowl for washing and a cup of nourishing stew.

When the men returned from fetching water they found the house in order.

CHAPTER THIRTEEN: THE NAMING

His First Year

Despite a custom requiring a new mother to remain in the house of her husband for the length of the cycle of the moon, Mary insisted on taking the child to the Temple. "If I can travel from Bethlehem to Jerusalem after giving birth," she reasoned, "I can travel a few steps into the city as well."

Her family had long ceased to argue with Mary.

Joseph carried the baby who had been bathed and wrapped in fresh linens. Anne was relieved that none they passed made note of Mary's presence as they walked along the path.

They entered the city through the Genneth Gate and followed the street beneath the Temple walls to the southern entrance. Joachim and Joseph entered the cleansing baths so that they could enter the inner Temple courtyards.

When they returned, the women followed the men as they climbed the stone steps to the triple gates and entered into the large tiled Courtyard of the Gentiles, the first of three courtyards that lay before the most sacred place: the Holiest of Holy where none could go but the highest of the High Priests.

The Courtyard of the Gentiles was filled with people and noise. Some visitors were preparing to enter deeper into the Temple. Others, having completed their prayers and offerings, were leaving the courtyard. Along one wall, moneychangers worked at tables. They traded temple coins for the gold and silver brought by pilgrims while merchants hawking doves threaded through the crowds.

Mary and Anne dared go no further. They had not yet been to the baths for cleansing and could not enter through the Gate Beautiful and into the second courtyard, the Courtyard of the Women. This was custom neither woman wished to ignore.

A peculiar woman rushed up to them, her garments billowing around her, her hands raised to the sky. Anne put herself between this wild looking one and Joseph who held the child.

Mary knew the woman. She was Anna, daughter of Phanuel. Anna was a prophetess who spent her days in the Temple fasting and praying. Mary had seen her many times. Mary took the baby from Joseph and held him out to Anna.

Joseph, Joachim and Anne gasped.

The woman prophet pushed out her hands in protest. "No. No. I am not worthy to hold one such as this. This is our Messiah, the promised one. He is come at last. He is come at last!" She whirled away from them. Her mantle fell away. A cloud of long, white curls burst out into the air around her head. She ran through the courtyard, shouting to all she passed, "I have seen him! I have seen him! The Lord my God!"

Anne grabbed the baby from Mary and handed him to Joseph.

Joachim followed Joseph, who carried the child through the Courtyard of the Women and into the Courtyard of Israel. There they presented the child for naming and circumcision.

Anne watched the old woman careening through the crowd. "Daughter, you would give your child to one such as that? You know not what you risk. Here in the Temple, one such as she might thrust your son into the hands of a priest, offering him up as if a dove purchased in the streets!"

Mary grew still and cold. She shut tight her lips. The pain of what was to come overwhelmed her. She sank to her knees. *My mother,* she realized, *is correct. I must take greater care. He is but a fragile babe.*

"Oh, my daughter," Anne sighed when she saw that Mary wept. She lifted her daughter to her feet and wrapped her arms around her. "Forgive me, child. I forget myself."

In the Courtyard of the Priests, an empty ornate chair sat waiting for the prophet Elijah. Joseph stood at one side of the chair. Joachim stood at the other with the baby in his arms.

The priest who had made the cut and bandaged the child prayed aloud. "Blessed be the Lord God of Abraham who has made us pure by his laws and given us circumcision."

Joseph responded. "He has purified us by his laws and has granted us to give our child into the covenant of Abraham our father. From this moment, this child shall be called Jesus, Emmanuel."

A righteous and devout man named Simeon saw the naming ceremony and went to them. He took Jesus from Joachim and was filled with a great peace. He held the baby high as if offering him to the Lord. He raised his eyes to the sky and prayed. "Now, Master, you may let your servant go in peace. As you have promised, my eyes have seen your salvation, a light for revelation to the gentiles and glory for your people Israel."

The old man's words frightened Joseph. He grabbed the child from Simeon. He and Joachim hurried away, but Simeon followed.

When the men and baby reached Mary and Anne, Simeon raised his hands in the air as if pleading with the Lord. "Behold, this child is destined for the fall and rise of many in Israel, and to be a sign that will be contradicted so that the thoughts of many hearts may be revealed." Having spoken, Simeon left them.

Grateful that neither Simeon nor Anna had drawn a crowd, Mary and her family hurried from the Temple and returned to the house of Joseph. Though Simeon's words were perplexing, they were soon forgotten in the happiness of the celebration that waited.

Neighbors stood at their gate bearing food, wine and gifts. One brought a flute, another a lyre. Together they ate, sang and danced to celebrate the naming of the new baby boy.

During the afternoon the baby was passed from hand-to-hand. All marveled at his strength and alertness. The men agreed that a fine big boy this one would be. The women approved of how robustly the baby took to breast. They assured Mary he was sure to sleep throughout the night before a new moon had risen.

Mary told none that when she changed the baby's bindings that she found him healed.

At sunset the lamps were lit and the celebration continued. The night grew late. The guests left and the women found their pallets. Joseph lightly touched Joachim's shoulder, "It is a favor I must ask of you."

"If it is within my power it is granted. What may I do for you?"

"While we were in Bethlehem, the child was given gifts, precious gifts. I have no safe place to bury them until the day he has need of such. Could you not keep them hidden in the hill?"

"Of course, Joseph. We will keep all safe."

"There are two chests. One contains gold coins, the other spices. I wrapped the chest in old tunics and have hidden them beneath hay at the back of my house where the animals are tethered." Carrying a lamp, he led Joachim to the chests.

Joachim squatted to examine them. He gasped when he saw that jewels were embedded in the top and sides of one. He dared not open it, but he could feel from the weight of it that it contained much gold. The other chest was made of gleaming mahogany with gold inlaid, carved flowers and vines flowing across its top and down its sides. The fragrance of Babylonian spices rose from it.

Joachim knew many people had seen these gifts fit for a king presented to Mary and Joseph. He felt cold fear run through his body as he wondered if thieves had followed them back to Jerusalem.

He hid the chests with the tunics and spread hay over them. Joachim took his rug and lay down beside the treasures. Joseph brought his rug and slept beside him.

The next morning Anne was relieved and thrilled to discover Naomi, the mid-wife, sitting at the gate in a donkey cart guided by Jude, the second son of Joachim.

Jude was relieved that Mother Anne showed no sign of the madness his brother Jacob had described. When Mary placed the child in his arms, Jude rejoiced. He smiled at Mary and said, "It is true."

"It is he," she answered. Retrieving the baby from Jude, she told him, "Go into the city with the men."

Joseph, Joachim and Jude walked to the market. They spoke of many things, of most the child. Finally, Joachim asked Joseph, "Do you remember the promise you made when we stood beside the table you made for my house?"

"Yes. I have not forgotten. As soon as Mary is healed we will be knocking on your gate. My Mary has a lovely view of the gardens climbing the hill before my house. I fear it is not enough. She longs for the fresh Galilean air."

"Joseph, there is work for you in Sepphoris and Nazareth. The hill is large and generous." Joachim leaned close to Joseph and whispered as if repeating a poorly kept secret, "Mother Anne would have me pack all your goods and drag you into the hills if she thought such a thing possible."

Joseph laughed. "I will keep my promise. Mary shall not disappear from your lives."

Jude spoke. "Though my sons Joses and James are yet babes, I beg you help form a bond between them and their new cousin."

"This shall be. They shall have many days together to climb the hill and chase rabbits from the brush."

While the men walked through the city market, Naomi carried out the duties for which she had been sent to the house of Joseph. Astonished at finding Mary healed, she fell silent and brooded. To an inquiry by Anne, she would say only that Mary was in good health.

Anne had no time to puzzle over Naomi's brief reply. She nearly danced around the courtyard as she watched Mary open the gifts from the house of Joachim that Jude had packed into the cart. There were stacks of soft cloths sent to bundle the baby. Bee balm in a small crock was sent to heal Mary's breasts. Balls of dyed wool sent ready for weaving.

Anne insisted that Mary retell each moment spent in Bethlehem. Together they rejoiced over the safe delivery of the child. At the end of the day, she and Naomi could recite the story without hesitation.

In the evening they sat in a circle in the courtyard and ate. The sun was not long out of the sky when the women were settled upon their pallets.

In the dark, Joachim and Jude pulled his carts to the place where the treasures lay hidden. With Joseph's help, they lifted the chests into the carts and stowed them beneath rugs.

The three men slept on the ground next to the carts.

Inside the house, Naomi turned on her pallet. She was certain she had missed something, for she knew no woman heals completely from the demands of birthing. Only after deciding she could insist upon a second examination could Naomi fall into a dreamless sleep.

Dreams troubled Anne. In them Mary withheld the child and turned away from her. She spoke with Naomi as if Anne did not exist. Anne woke, afraid for her daughter.

She lit a wick and climbed to the loft where Mary and Jesus lay sleeping. When she saw how peaceful they lay, Anne chastised herself for being foolish. Her daughter and grandson were well. What more could she wish? "Forgive me, Yahweh," she whispered.

Anne returned to her pallet and continued to beg forgiveness for her lack of faith until a deep, heavy sleep overcame her.

CHAPTER FOURTEEN: THE IRE OF HEROD

His First Year

The men who followed the great star failed to return to Herod. His soldiers were unable to find the visitors from lands to the East of Judea, returning only with stories of people lining the paths of Bethlehem to honor a newly born King of the Jews.

While Jerusalem slept, a drunken Herod wept and trembled in the arms of his concubine. Sobbing, he told her, "My wives and children spin webs of deceit around me. The Sanhedrin constantly scheme to increase their power in Jerusalem. The high priest conspires with the moneychangers to hide riches flowing into the Temple while I empty my money chests to build a great city.

"The people of Judea threaten me on all sides. And now this," he wept and pulled at his beard, "now this! They speak of a new King. A new King of the Jews! I tell you these people will rise up and murder me. I am ruined! I am ruined," he bawled.

The woman in his bed tried to comfort him. She pulled him close and laid his head upon her breasts.

Inside Herod a fierce rage began to spin like a waterspout growing at sea. His anger swamped him. He drew his knees to his chest and with both feet shoved the woman from his bed. He heard the pop of her skull cracking on the marble floor. Ignoring the moaning woman lying in the growing pool of blood, Herod rose from his bed and roared, "Dresser!"

The servant who slept at the door of the chamber ran into the room. His eyes bulged at the sight of the dying woman. He wanted to help her, but his terror of Herod kept him from approaching her. He bowed his head, "Sire."

Ignoring the man cowering at the door, naked Herod paced the room. His face turned red. He screamed at the walls.

"I am Herod. I am the King. I am the one to be feared. There is no new King!"

Herod whirled to face the servant. He grew calm. An ugly smile spread across his face.

The servant trembled as he watched the man before him. He knew this calm. It meant dangerous action would follow. He dared not move.

The woman ceased her moaning and lay deathly still.

Herod heeded neither servant nor concubine. He was thinking of his special Centuria housed in barracks west of the city.

Under a threat of another Jewish uprising he had persuaded Caesar to send him additional soldiers. He had been insulted upon their arrival. Caesar had sent, not a Roman Centuria, but an Auxiliary Centuria. Eighty mercenaries from the far flung reaches of the Roman Empire, not even their officers Roman. His jagged laughter filled the room rising to the high ceilings. "Isis smiles upon me. These are exactly the men I need," he shouted.

Herod remembered the servant. "Get me a tunic," he demanded. Looking at the woman who had shared his bed, he laughed, "a blood red one."

"Yes, master." The servant ran to a side chamber where hundreds of silk tunics hung on pegs. He grabbed the first red colored garment he saw and ran back to Herod. With shaking hands he helped Herod dress.

Herod flung the servant into the wall. "Call the Commander of my Legion. Send him to my parapet."

The servant pushed off from the wall, anxious to obey and grateful to escape the mad man before him. He moved quickly toward the doorway.

"Wait!" Herod commanded.

The servant froze in place, daring not to look into the eyes of his master.

Herod voice was calm. "Pour wine for me before you go."

The servant rushed to a table beneath a window and with shaking hands lifted a golden pitcher. He poured wine into a jeweled cup and carried it to Herod.

Herod took the cup and kicked at the servant. "Get out!" he snarled.

The servant fled, racing to fulfill his orders.

Herod drank deeply. The taste of fine wine made him feel sober. He staggered out of his chambers to the steps leading to his favorite tower. He steadied himself by leaning against the smooth marble walls as he climbed upward. At times he grabbed the gold encrusted balustrade to keep from falling.

He stepped out into the night air, his red tunic blowing around him like the garment of a dancer. A surprised guard jumped to attention. Herod ignored him. He walked to the edge and leaned upon the parapet wall.

Herod looked to the south. The sun was beginning to bring light into the sky. Though still in shadows, Herod could see the old city, the City of David. He laughed, imagining the great King David looking at his city as it lay below him this night.

Once beautiful, the old city was crowded and filthy. At the far end, the Dung Gate led to great piles of garbage thrown from Jerusalem year after year into the Hinnom Valley. Acres of burning land smoldered, sending a vile stench into the air above the southeastern quadrant of Jerusalem.

Herod laughed, raised his cup to toast King David and filled his mouth with wine. He would make it his city, the city of Herod.

To his right, the upper city climbed the hill spreading out before his palace. Herod again raised his cup, this time in toast to citizens of Jerusalem living in fine houses with beautifully walled, landscaped courtyards and ornately tile-floored rooms.

He leaned over the parapet and shouted, "You do not fool me. You wear false faces and curry my favor while you hate and fear me. Fear me you must for I am the King of the Jews. Do not be mistaken, my duplicitous friends, there will be no other!"

To himself he whispered, "My city, my city from end to end. No one will take it from me. No one will take it from me." He screamed to the sky, "No one! Not even this so called baby King!"

The Commander of the Army of Caesar in Judea stood at the steps, watching the barefoot Herod staggering on the parapet. *How,* he wondered, *had Caesar come to be so taken in by this fool? Not even a beautiful seaside city built in his name could convince the Centurion to trust one such as this!*

He did not rush to Herod, nor did he bow. He was Roman. He did the bidding of this one only at the command of Caesar. The Cohort Commander took one step out of the doorway. "Greetings King Herod. I received a message you have need of me."

Herod turned away from the wall. He studied the Roman. His face revealed contempt for this man he deemed another arrogant fool from Rome with whom he must deal. He spoke as if an old friend stood before him. "Greetings Commander. I welcome you to my palace." He smiled. "I have a special task that requires a certain, um, shall I say, talent?"

A gust of wind swirled around Herod, sending into the air the curly ends of his long hair. The skirt of his tunic billowed upward exposing his naked loins. He gestured for the Roman to come close.

The Centurion did not move. He asked, "Such talent would be?"

Herod modulated his voice to seem truly concerned with the welfare of the Commander. "There is no need to bother you with details. It is a small matter, much too small for one as occupied as you with keeping my city safe," he said, emphasizing the word "my."

"It is but a simple mission," he continued. "I believe the Auxiliary Century now housed in your barracks can manage the task." Herod, turning his back to the Roman, allowed contempt to sound in his voice, "I am certain you need no reminder that these soldiers were sent for my use by Caesar himself."

Unimpressed, the Commander replied without troubling to veil his intended sarcasm, "Require you the presence here in your palace of the entire Auxiliary Century? Or will the Commander of the Auxiliary be satisfactory?"

Herod turned to face the Roman and leaned against the parapet wall. He controlled his anger. He would not lower himself to engage in petty quarrelling with one such as this. Scorn seeped from his voice as he replied, "How generous of you to offer to escort eighty men to my quarters. The Auxiliary Commander will do." He turned his back on the Roman officer and tersely ordered, "Have him here within the hour."

"So be it," said the relieved Roman. He left without saluting Herod. Troubling questions played in his head as he descended the stairs. What could possibly require these nocturnal orders? What madness does this man now scheme? No good shall come of this. He mentally shrugged. If he thinks I am offended that he asks for soldiers other than mine, he is even a greater fool than I have thought.

The Cohort Commander left the palace. A guard with a lit torch awaited him on the street. The Commander nodded to the guard. "Go," he ordered.

When they reached the fortress, a rider was sent to the military camp set up west of the city. Within the hour the Commander of the auxiliary force was standing on the parapet high above the city receiving whispered instructions from King Herod.

CHAPTER FIFTEEN: SAFE PASSAGE

His First Year

Again an angel came to Joseph as he slept. "Rise, do not delay. Herod plots to find and destroy the child. Take the child and his mother. Flee to Egypt. Stay there until I tell you to return."

Joseph woke whispering the words, "So be it." He rose. He made no sound as he stepped away from the sleeping Joachim and Jude. He untethered his donkey, patted it and whispered assurances to the animal as he led him to the gate. On the road, Joseph tied his donkey to a thorn bush.

He reentered the courtyard and quickly collected items for their journey. He threw two sleeping rugs over the back of the donkey and hung over them a single rope, a wineskin and a leather water pouch tied to each end. He filled a cloth bag with bread and tied it to the rope where it crossed the animal's back. He collected his tools, bagged them and placed them on the ground next to his donkey.

In the house he found Anne curled upon her pallet sleeping so deeply as to be undisturbed by the snoring of Naomi. He slipped up the ladder and found Mary awake, her eyes wide and questioning. Placing a finger before his closed lips, he signaled her to speak not. He motioned for her to pass the baby to him and to gather up her things.

Mary collected cloths and a small amount of clothing, including her dowry mantle upon which Anne had sewn silver coins. She rolled them into a bundle, which she flung over her back, tying the ends at her neck.

Joseph carried Jesus down the ladder and led Mary to the door. When Mary stopped by her mother, he touched her arm and shook his head from side to side, warning her to wake not Anne.

Mary took the baby from Joseph and followed him from the house and through the gate. Standing by the donkey, she whispered, "Why, Joseph? Why must we leave in the night like thieves? Why can I not say farewell to my mother and father?"

He pulled her farther from the gate. His voice was quiet, but firm. "The angel spoke to me. He says we must flee the wrath of King Herod. We must not delay. We will safe in Egypt."

"Egypt? Joseph that is so distant! The road is full of danger. How can we be safe from Herod on the road? Surely we can find a safer place here to hide."

Joseph grabbed Mary by her shoulders forcing her to stand still before him. He leaned forward and growled into her ear, "Mary, be quiet. Do as I say." He released her and picked up the bag containing his carpentry tools. With his right hand he grabbed the neck of the bag and lifted it onto his back. In his left hand he took the rope thrown round the donkey's neck. He led the animal away from his house.

The terrified Mary followed, carrying the baby in her arms, his head close to her neck. Tears slipped down her face. Never before had Joseph been harsh with her. "Please," she begged, "leave a message for my parents. They must know why we have left them."

They made one stop before they turned off the lane before the house of Joseph. Mary watched from the gate as Joseph roused a neighbor from his bed. She saw them hold a quick, whispered conversation. The door closed in Joseph's face and he returned to her. "Come," he said quietly.

They passed beyond their small enclave and turned south on the broad road leading past the city. The road was rough.

Dark clouds covered the moon. Mary walked behind Joseph. Neither spoke.

When they were past the walls of the city where the road dropped down into the Hinnom Valley, a dark cloud parted above them revealing two immense angels with sky black wings. One shrouded the donkey and vanished. The other wrapped his wings around Mary, Joseph and Jesus.

Mary felt air rush past and heard her baby laugh as they were lifted into the sky. Blackness overcame them. They slept, cradled in the angel's wings, as they swept over unwary Bethlehem, Hebron, Beersheba, the Valley of Salt and the edge of the Great Sea.

At dawn they woke and found that they, along with Joseph's donkey, had been left on a road leading to a Nabatean farming village in Nile River Delta.

CHAPTER SIXTEEN: LOSS

His First Year

Sunlight brought Anne awake with a sudden start. Her heart beat wildly against her ribs. When she saw that Mary and the child were gone, she ran from the house, calling for her husband.

Anne was shaking the boy sleeping at the open gate when Jude and Joachim reached her. Joachim pulled Anne away and began to question the boy. "Why lie you here?"

The boy jumped up and began to stutter. "I... I... I... please sir, do not beat me. The carpenter begged my father send me to lie here so that in the light of day I might deliver to you his words."

He held his arm before his face as if expecting blows. When none came, he dropped his arm and continued, "I am to tell you that Joseph has taken his family away to protect the child. He says they will return when it is safe. He asks that you close up his house and bar it against thieves. These are his exact words."

"Gone?" Anne was stunned. She wailed, "My Mary and my precious grandson gone? How is this? Two days. I have had only two days with my child." She wanted to fling herself upon Joseph and claw at his eyes. How could he leave with no farewell? She turned to her husband and pleaded, "Joachim, go for them."

Jude grabbed the boy, lifting him off his feet and pulling his face close to his own. "Which way did they go?" he demanded.

"I know not," the boy cried and began to shake.

Joachim pulled Jude away from the boy. "Son, son. Do no harm to this one. He is only a messenger." To the boy, he said, "No harm will come to you as long as you are certain Joseph had no other words for us."

"Sir, I have told you all that my father has asked me to report."

"Did you see the way they turned from the gate?"

"No, sir. He came in the night to the house of my father. I was asleep when he came. He was gone when my father woke me and sent me here."

Naomi, awakened by the commotion at the gate, watched from the door. Fear glistened in her eyes.

"Wife, we must trust that Joseph has valid reason to take away his family. He would not leave us in such a way without good cause."

Jude begged his father, "Let me search for them. I will bring them back."

"They have been gone far too long and there are too many streets they may have turned down. We have lost much this night. Do not ask me to lose you as well." He saw Jude's disappointment, but held fast. "Pack the carts. Douse the fire and board up the house. We know not the danger that drove them away. We must not linger here. I will speak with the father of this boy. I will not be long."

Joachim placed his hand on the boy's shoulder. "Show me the way."

Anne dropped to her knees. "Dear Lord God of Abraham, return my husband with news of where my child and her precious son have gone. Bring them back to me this day." Even as she begged, she knew in her heart this would be a prayer unanswered.

Naomi and Anne collected a few items from the house.

Jude shuttered the windows. He was nailing the gate shut when Joachim returned. They turned to him.

Joachim shook his head and said, "The father of the boy could tell me nothing of the intentions of Joseph. We must trust that Joseph will send a message." He pulled a knife from the folds of his girdle and carved upon the boards of the gate: House of Joseph.

Jude and Joachim led the donkey-pulled carts. Wearing a mantle the color of peaches left behind by Mary, Anne followed with Naomi at her side. The saddened group left the street upon which the house of Joseph stood, stepped upon the broad road and turned to the north.

When they were well out of the city and felt the road rising into the hills, Naomi signaled Anne to fall back out of the hearing of the men. "Anne, you know that I have many years as a midwife. And you know my reputation. I am always the first sent for."

Anne could only nod in assent. Her face paled. Fear gripped her. Had the midwife found something terrible?

"I fear saying this to you. You will think I have gone mad."

"Oh, dear Lord God of Abraham," Anne whispered as she gripped Naomi's arm. "What is it?"

"Anne, Mary is..." she hesitated and then words came rushing out, "Mary is like a virgin. How can this be? I examined her carefully. She was as if a pure maiden."

Color rushed back into Anne's face. Laughter of relief escaped her throat. "Woman, you gave me such a fright! Have you forgotten the angel Gabriel came to Mary? Have you forgotten this is the Son of God she has borne?" The words echoed in her mind as she spoke them: *The Son of God. The Son of God.*

The midwife threw up her arms. "Anne, Anne, you do not know of the stories I have heard. In the face of great sin, people say many strange things. I am sorry. I did not believe the angel came to Mary, but now..."

"Have you still doubt, woman?"

"No. I have seen for myself. There is no trick man can do to heal a woman so. It must be the work of Yahweh. Please forgive your friend."

Anne wrapped her arms around Naomi, her words more bravely spoken than felt. "It is a miraculous event. We are blessed to be part of it. Do not waste your energy on remorse. Let us rejoice together and pray that their safe return will not be long in coming."

Yahweh was with the travelers. They returned to the Nazarean hills saddened but unharmed and unaware that behind them the blood of children flowed.

CHAPTER SEVENTEEN: EGYPT

His First Years

The Nabateans, pushed south by the Romans, spoke Arabic and welcomed Jews who fled the tyrants. Joseph found an abandoned one-room house with a walled courtyard. The talent of a carpenter was valued and none in the village objected to their use of it.

The coins from Mary's dowry mantle enabled them to shop in the market for clay pots, wood, grain and wine. By the end of the first day, their house was established.

Joseph turned his wood-working skills to the making of farming implements. These he bartered for a hand mill, a loom and wool.

They quickly fell into a daily routine. Joseph left the village with the men who tilled the soil and worked beside them. He mended plows and yokes. At times he planted and weeded.

Mary went daily to the well. She longed to join in the lively conversations carried on by the women as they waited to fill their jars, but Joseph had warned her to speak to none. Mary obeyed, offering only polite greetings.

At first, the women thought her shy; later, some thought her rude. In the weeks that followed, busy with their own chores, most came to ignore her. None, however, could ignore the beauty of her woven tunics.

Mary was lonely, but took solace in watching her son grow. He was a happy baby who filled his parents with joy. He endured none of the illnesses that so often overtook infants. He was unusually strong. He stood and walked without holding her hand before the first anniversary of his birth. Shortly afterward, he began to speak. His parents were amazed. His words were not those of a baby not yet weaned, but those of a thoughtful schoolboy.

Joseph feared that revealing the boy's great intellect would put them at risk. He insisted Jesus speak not in the presence of others. He insisted Mary keep Jesus away from other children.

More than one woman doing laundry at the edge of the Nile noted how protective of Jesus was Mary. They slapped their clothes against the rocks and shook their heads. "Spoils him," they whispered, "this shall bring her many regrets."

At first, those who knew Mary and Joseph thought their boy shy. Later, when he continued to be silent, they thought him mute and wondered what great sin his parents had committed to bring such a burden upon the child. Some began to avoid their company.

Mary felt their disapproval and her separation from all women. She longed for her family and to be in the Nazarean hills. She was surprised when a young woman named Miriam approached her at the well.

"I have heard you have great skill at the loom. I am to be wed and I wish to have a new garment to wear to the house of my husband. My father can provide the wool. My father also says he will supply you with figs and grapes for a year."

Mary was charmed by the enthusiasm of Miriam. It pleased her to learn that her weaving was a topic of flattering talk in the village. She smiled at the young woman, "It is an honor to be asked to weave for you."

With her water jar on her head and Jesus at her side, Mary returned to the house of Joseph, considering Miriam's request as she walked. The whole village would attend the wedding. The bride's tunic must truly be a work of art. Before she reached her doorstep Mary knew how she would turn rough wool into a soft, gossamer garment worthy of such an occasion.

Mary spent many days weaving and sewing the wedding tunic from wool she dyed lilac with diluted juice of grapes. When it was finished, she left a message at the well.

Within the day Miriam and her servant stood at the gate. Miriam called, "Peace be with you."

Mary went to the window. "Peace also to you and welcome to this house. I regret I must ask you to wait at my gate. My husband insists that I keep it locked in his absence."

Mary turned away from the window and spoke to Jesus who sat on the floor playing a numbers game with rocks. "Run with me," Jesus grabbed the sleeve of Mary's tunic and they ran out of the house.

Mary unlatched the gate and embraced Miriam. "Please come inside. There I will bathe your feet and give you drink." To the servant she said, "Come and stay by the door in the shade of the house. I will give you drink. I have bread in the pan and figs in the bowl."

Mary led Miriam into a cool room. She placed before Miriam a soft cloth and large, shallow bowl nearly full of water. Taking Jesus with her, she tended to the servant, delivering to him a fig wrapped in flat bread, as well as a gourd filled with water.

"May God bless you and this household," the servant said as he accepted the food and drink.

"And so to you many blessings," Mary replied.

Anxious to see her wedding tunic, Miriam had washed herself in Mary's absence and refused Mary's offer of food and drink. She gasped when Mary unfolded a tunic that seemed made of the pale violet light of early evening. "Mary," Miriam exclaimed, "never have I seen such beautiful cloth! This is fit for the wife of a king."

Mary was delighted. "This was a task of love my friend. You have given me much joy by allowing me to prepare this special garment for you. May I drape it over you, so we can be certain of the fit?"

Mary watched the maiden turn in the light and airy tunic, causing its hem to lift and swirl. In a bittersweet moment, she saw herself dancing wrapped in the beautiful cloth. She remembered her girlish dreams of flowers sprinkled before her as she walked behind her new husband Joseph. She longed for the dancing and laughter that never filled a week of her marriage celebration.

Her pain for moments unspent was quickly pushed away by the joy Mary saw in the face of Miriam. "Come, dear. Remove the garment and I shall wrap it carefully so that no harm can come to it."

The betrothed girl hugged herself. "Oh, how I wish I might wear this forever. Mary, in it I feel beautiful. I shall outshine my groom."

Mary helped Miriam pull the tunic over her head and redress. She rolled the wedding tunic in her own blue mantel.

As she took the packet, Miriam extended an invitation. "Mary, on my marriage day, my servant will come for you. Your family will sit in a place of honor. So fine is your work, I know of no other way to repay you."

"I am touched. We look forward to sharing the celebration of your new life. This is my gift to you, please accept it as such."

Words gushed from the excited maiden. "My mother will be filled with joy when she sees my wedding tunic. We must find a truly beautiful mantle to wear with it. I must leave. Forgive me for not staying longer, but despite the presence of my servant, and despite not leaving the village walls, my mother grows anxious when I am out of her sight."

Mary took the hand of Jesus in hers. Together they led Miriam to the door. The servant rose and followed the two women and the child to the gate.

Miriam handed her package to her servant with orders to handle it with much care. She and Mary embraced.

Jesus waved goodbye as they hurried away. "You have made the woman happy, mother."

Mary smiled.

That evening after Joseph had eaten and the boy lay sleeping, Mary told Joseph of her visitors.

Joseph listened carefully. He asked, "Did Jesus speak to the woman or her servant?"

"No, I am sure of it. He was with me every moment. And, husband, she was thrilled with her tunic. She paid the boy no heed."

"I am glad for you, Mary, that she was pleased with your work. You must be more careful not to arouse attention. Weave no more for any but our family."

Mary turned away so that Joseph would not see her tears.

She had not meant to put her family at risk. Mary yearned for her parents and the company of those she could trust.

As promised, the servant came to announce the date of the wedding celebration. Mary grew excited as the day neared. But she was not to see Miriam dance in the violet tunic covered by the very mantel in which Mary had wrapped it.

When it was time to bring the guests to the village square, the servant of Miriam who came for the family of Joseph found an open gate and an empty house.

CHAPTER EIGHTEEN: EXODUS

His Fifth Year

News of the death of Herod was slow to reach the village where Mary and Joseph had found refuge. It was said that Archelaus, son of Herod the Great, newly ruled in Judea and his brother Antipas ruled in Galilee. It was said they ruled with not as heavy hand as did their father.

Mary pleaded with Joseph to join the small caravan of Jewish refugees forming to return to their homeland.

Worried that the sons of Herod carried on the search for Jesus, Joseph waited for a sign. On the eve of the departure of the caravan, the angel spoke to Joseph. "Take the boy and return to Judea." Joseph woke Mary and told her to prepare.

Mary did not object to being again roused in the night. She bundled long loaves of bread and an iron pan into a thick woven cloth to carry on her back. She filled three small water bags for she, Joseph and Jesus to strap to their sides. She filled with nuts the pockets of Jesus and Joseph's tunics. She filled her own pockets with small wooden cups. She gave to Joseph the few remaining coins from her dowry mantle.

Joseph wrapped his carpentry tools in a rug and tied it to his donkey's back. Atop it he piled hay. Over that he threw a large goatskin water bag and a finely woven bag full of grain.

A crowd of people from the village waited at the road to say farewell, praying to the Lord God of Abraham that the refugees would have a journey safe from thieves or worse. Few believed such a thing possible. Friends wept and kissed goodbye.

Joseph's family was the last to join those brave enough to leave the safety of the village. Mary walked behind Joseph with Jesus at her side. Joseph held the donkey's lead. In a few minutes the caravan spread out in a jagged line along the road.

Their many days of walking began. They walked until the midday heat forced them to stop. If they could not find trees under which to rest, they tied large cloths to branches they used as walking sticks and lay beneath the triangles of shade.

They walked from mid-afternoon until dusk. When the sun fell from the sky, they built a fire, shared their food, set a guard and dropped upon pallets.

In the darkest time of night, the silent boy Jesus walked among the sleeping travelers. When the sun sent faint light into the sky, all woke refreshed and strong.

Their water bags did not go dry. They met with no harm, nor threat of harm. None fell ill, nor fell behind. In the villages along the road they were given food and wine.

Daily they sent prayers of thanksgiving to the Lord God of Abraham. They said to each other, "Yahweh is with us."

They walked along the edge of the Great Sea. They walked through desert. When they reached Gaza they rejoiced and kissed the ground and turned to the east to find their way through the rugged Judean hills.

Joseph and his family separated from the others at the village of En Karem. There lived John, the son of Zechariah the husband of Mary's beloved Elizabeth.

As was his habit, now that he was too old to carry out Priestly duties, Zechariah squatted on a small rug beneath a tree near the gate of his courtyard. There he watched his son play and greeted all who passed by on the road.

The boy was a wild child who liked to climb the courtyard wall and leap from it as if he had wings. To his parents it seemed he moved every waking moment. They learned to feel no alarm when he would abruptly drop to the ground and fall into a deep sleep. Often Zechariah carried John into his house and laid him upon a pallet.

John spoke little, which worried his mother. Zechariah could see that the boy understood all that transpired about him. He thought it not a bad thing to listen more than talk. He was surprised when John's shouting broke through his reverie.

"Father, father, they come!" John stood atop the courtyard wall and pointed to the curve in the road. "They have come!" He leaped onto the bricked road.

"John, John, who comes? Come back here!" Zechariah called out as he rose from the ground and hobbled after his son. When he saw Mary was the woman who approached, he was filled with delight.

Jesus ran ahead of his parents. When he reached John they embraced, instantly feeling their unique bond. It was as if they were joined in the womb and had never been apart. They kissed and ran to Zechariah who held them close, an arm around each.

By the open gate, Elizabeth leaned upon a walking stick, waving and laughing. "Hurry, hurry, my heart is bursting to hold you."

Mary, Joseph and the donkey caught up with Zechariah and the boys.

Zechariah, though still in the embrace of the children, remembered his manners. "Peace be with you," he greeted, laughing as he spoke.

"And, also to you," answered Joseph.

The boys pulled away from Zechariah and ran to Elizabeth.

"Beautiful, beautiful," she murmured as she knelt to gather Jesus into her arms.

He smiled and kissed her forehead. "Peace to this household," he said to her.

John stood back, watching and smiling. He felt as if he had presented his mother with a great and wonderful gift.

After greeting and embracing Zechariah, Mary ran to her cousin.

"How is it that you honor our house?" asked Elizabeth as the women held each other.

"Now that King Herod is dead, we return to the house of my husband. We could not pass by so near and not seek you. Are you well?"

Elizabeth stepped away from Mary, ignoring her question. She was an old woman full of aches and pains. She considered none worthy of discussion. "Where have you been? No one has heard of you for too long. Your mother weeps at this moment. Let us go inside. Let us give you drink. And food, of course! You must be hungry, for you look as if you have journeyed long."

They did appear as weary travelers. The hems of their tunics were reddish-brown from the dust on the road. The donkey sagged as if he could not carry his burdens one more step.

Joseph refused to enter the courtyard until he had water to wash his feet and sandals.

Mary removed her sandals and followed Elizabeth into the house. She instructed Jesus to remain in the courtyard.

Elizabeth ordered her servant to prepare a meal. She brought water to Mary and washed her feet. The servant brought water to drink. Mary sipped from the gourd, dipped the edge of her mantle into it and wiped her face.

The men joined them and soon the house was full of excited talk as Mary and Joseph told the story of their exile.

Outside, with a single jump, Jesus joined John atop the courtyard wall.

"You leap like a lion. Can you also fly like a bird?"

"Perhaps," Jesus teased.

They sat, legs dangling, feet kicking the wall. "I have waited long for you, my cousin. Is now the time?"

"No, John. We must be patient. My father in heaven will tell us when to act. For now, he wishes us to be children and obey our parents."

"So be it." John was relieved. He did not feel ready to fulfill the purpose for which God made him. He questioned Jesus no more of their future. Instead, he asked, "What else can you do beside leap walls?"

"Many things that will surprise you."

"Show me."

"Take me to water." Jesus floated off the wall onto the road.

Laughing, John jumped after him. They ran to the village well. John pulled up the water bag and filled a large leather bucket.

Jesus told him to pour the water upon the ground. When the water was drawn onto the ground, Jesus dipped his hands into the muddy spot. From the wet soil he deftly sculpted a sparrow. He put the clay bird into the hands of his cousin.

John was astonished. He saw that each feather was in its rightful place. He saw the feathers take on color. He felt the cold clay become warm and the tiny claws of the sparrow scratch the palms of his hands. He opened his hands, palms raised to the sky. The bird flew into a nearby tree and began to chirp.

John bent with laughter. "Do it again," he pleaded.

Jesus looked about. A woman carrying a water jug approached. "No, John, I cannot."

"So be it. Let us return to the house of my father."

They held hands and walked the dusty path and back to the courtyard.

Their parents, engaged in intense conversation, were unaware they had been absent.

Mary, Joseph, and Jesus stayed three days with Elizabeth, Zechariah and John. When they were fully rested, Joseph again loaded the donkey. Promising to meet in Jerusalem at Passover, they departed for the house of Joseph only a half-day's walk from En Karem.

As Elizabeth stood at her gate watching them leave, she realized that she was free of pain. She saw too that her husband stood straight, as if he were a young man.

When Mary, Joseph and Jesus reached the garden area outside the northern wall of Jerusalem, they stood in stunned silence.

The small Jewish enclave was no more. The houses lay in piles of rubble. The well had been torn apart and filled with stones.

Mary wept at the agony of loss rising from the debris. Jesus stood beside her and reached up for her hand. He too grieved for those friends and neighbors who had joined in the celebration of his naming.

Joseph moved amid the broken mud bricks lying scattered where his house had stood. Not a plank of wood remained. He could see by the thickness of the thorny vines climbing through the ruins that much time had passed since his house had been looted and destroyed.

He silently prayed that Joachim and Anne had left long before the soldiers came to do the dirty work of Herod. He wondered where his neighbors had gone and if he would see any again. He feared he would not.

"Mary, I am sorry, but our travels are not over. I think we must travel north to Galilee. I have heard Antipas rules there with a lighter hand than does Archelaus. Away from Judea, we may find it easier to keep the boy safe."

"Please, Joseph, let us go to the house of my father. We will be safe hidden in the hill."

"Yes, Mary. We shall go there." He did not share his dark thoughts that Joachim and Anne may have been caught in the same attack that ruined his house. "Come, we must not tarry here."

Joseph tugged on the rope around the neck of the donkey. They retraced their steps along the path beside the northernmost wall of Jerusalem. When they reached the place where the wall turned south and the road continued north, Joseph stopped and looked back, silently vowing that he would reclaim the land upon which his house had stood.

They began the long walk up into the Nazarene hills.

That night they found a house with lamp lit and were welcomed, fed and given mats upon which to sleep.

On the second day, when they had been upon the road long enough for the sun to reach mid-point in the sky, they saw across the road a man dressed in richly embroidered, flowing robes walking toward them.

Joseph observed the exceedingly long blue fringes along the edges of the man's mantle. When he saw that the man had a small box containing scriptures bound to his forehead, Joseph knew this man to be a Pharisee.

The Pharisee stopped suddenly and peered into a ditch. He shuddered at what he saw and ran across the road. As he hurried past them, he pulled a scented cloth from the sleeve of his tunic and waved it before his face.

"What, husband, do you think this man has seen to make him rush past us as if we were invisible?"

Joseph shook his head. "I know not. Yet, I would think, God has blessed us by sparing us his acquaintance."

Before they could stop him, Jesus ran ahead and crossed the road at the exact place they had seen the man compelled to flee. On the ground there appeared to be a pile of dirty rags lying in the ditch. Jesus reached down and pulled a bloody cloth away, revealing the face of a badly beaten man.

"What is it?" Mary called. "What have you found?

"A man," Jesus answered.

"Be careful, he may be a leper!" Mary warned.

Ignoring his mother, Jesus crouched upon his knees and whispered into the bleeding ear of the fallen man. "You will sleep only a short while longer. When you wake you will be healed. Do not seek revenge. Go to the Temple and thank the Lord God of Abraham that you have been saved."

He touched the unconscious man. The blood ran back into him and his broken bones mended.

Jesus crossed the road and waited for Joseph and Mary who were quickly at his side. "Mother," Jesus said, "this man was beaten and I think robbed. He will be well when he wakes." Then he turned to Joseph. "Have we Temple coin to put in his pocket?"

Joseph retrieved from the folds of his girdle two silver half shekels of Tyre and gave them to Jesus.

Jesus returned to the sleeping man and placed the coins in one hand and curled his fingers around them. He ran back to his parents.

It was a hard walk up into the hill country. So anxious were they to reach the house of Joachim, they did not stop until darkness threatened. Their progress often was slowed by a need to step off the road.

They stood aside as caravans from Damascus passed carrying to Jerusalem markets exotic fruits, cloths made with gold and silver threads and other rare and valuable goods. For walkers, it was move or be overrun as they watched men wearing swords with curved, gleaming blades move up and down the caravan on impatient horses. The camel drivers paid no attention to travelers. Jesus loved seeing the huge camels stride by as if it were feathers they carried rather than heavy bags and trunks. He laughed when he saw one spit on its keeper.

When they were hungry, Joseph plucked grain from the corners of valley fields, careful to avoid being cut by tares entwined about the barley stalks in these plots, left untended to feed those upon the road. He picked olives and figs from trees beside the road. In each village through which they passed, they refilled their water bags.

An occasional rider, intent upon an important mission, swept past on a fast horse.

As they neared the fertile valley below Nazareth, a troop of Roman soldiers marched toward them, filling the road. Mary pulled Jesus into a ditch at the edge of the road.

The scarlet mantel of the Centurion was thrown over golden plates of armor that glistened in the sunlight. His troops stopped behind him when he drew hard upon the reins controlling his glossy black stallion.

Mary and Joseph stared at the ground, but Jesus looked straight into the eyes of the Roman.

The soldiers grew uneasy as they watched the horse dance before these three unimposing people.

Joseph drew Jesus close to him.

Jesus could feel Joseph tremble.

Mary held her breath fearing the sound of her moving lungs would antagonize the Roman.

Jesus smiled at the Roman.

The soldier laughed. This boy has spirit. He could make a good soldier one day. He kicked his horse and cantered away, signaling his troops to move forward.

And so it was that they traveled. On the forth day after leaving the ruins of the house of Joseph, Mary saw her mother.

Anne was at the well, bringing up water, when she heard the bray of the donkey outside her courtyard wall. The sight of Jesus running toward her took away her breath. His sun-darkened skin gleamed and curls danced about his face. She saw that his body was sturdy and perfect.

"Peace to you, Grandmother," he called out as he ran to Anne, his sweet voice a song carried to her ears on a soft breeze.

Anne dropped to her knees and wrapped her arms around Him. "Jesus, Jesus, happy are my eyes to look upon you! Happy are my ears to hear your voice." She held him close to her breast as long as he would allow.

Remembering the water-filled gourd in her hand, she asked, "Dear child, may I give you drink?"

Without a word, he took the gourd and drank.

Mary and Joseph entered the courtyard. "Mother, we could not hold him back, he was so excited to see you." Mary laughed and hugged her mother, the two enclosing Jesus in their embrace. The women leaned away from each other, eyes exchanging the unspoken agony of separation.

Jesus squirmed out of their embrace and ran to Joseph as he entered the courtyard.

In the happiness of seeing her daughter and grandson safe, Anne forgot her vow never to forgive Joseph. "Ah, Joseph," Anne greeted, "Peace to you and may God bless you all the days of your life for keeping safe my daughter and this precious child."

"Peace be with you, dear Mother Anne."

"Please, Joseph, allow me to bring water." Anne ran to well and drew more water by pulling up a goatskin bucket.

Joseph took the gourd from the hands of Jesus and joined Anne at the well. "Your hospitality is always generous. Are we not family? I can take care of myself." He took the bucket from Anne. "Go to your daughter. I shall drink and then seek out Joachim."

"I have freshly cooked round bread and broth still warm from breakfast. Surely you will allow me to give you food." It was a statement, not a question.

Mary laughed. "Oh, mother, allow Joseph go to my father."

Joseph added, "Mary is right. I truly do not hunger for food; but for the company of Joachim, Jesus and I are starved."

Anne waved Joseph away with both hands. "So be it. Leave! You will find him among the olive trees below us." She turned to Mary. "Do you need to rest? Are you hungry? What may I do for you?"

"Let us go into your garden, Mother. There we will talk. Where are my sisters?"

"They are beating the trees. The olives are ready to drop and the crop is abundant. Tomorrow we will take them to be pressed."

CHAPTER NINETEEN: EDEN

His Fifth Year

Mary and Anne were not long in the garden when they heard the sound of laughter coming from the courtyard. As soon as Joseph found him, Joachim had called for all to cease their labors and return to his house in the hill to celebrate the return of his daughter.

Mary turned at the sound of the garden gate. She ran to meet her father, who carried Jesus on his shoulders. "Papa, Papa!"

"My daughter, my daughter," he laughed and swept her into a dance.

Ester and Marta followed. They pulled Mary away from Joachim. They embraced her and kissed her face. They took her into the courtyard where others of her family gathered.

Waiting for her were David and his sons, Ezra and Eyal; Jude and his wife, Ora; and Jacob and his wife Mary, who was new to the house of Joachim. Jacob's wife held on her hip a boy child, not yet old enough to walk.

Mary took the boy from her and he laughed. "This is a happy child. You are blessed."

"His name is John. He is a happy child. As now is this household. All have long waited your return."

"I have longed to be here."

Mary stiffened and turned to survey the courtyard. "Hava? Where is my Hava?"

Marta answered. "Hava is married and lives in the house of her husband in Nazareth."

"Hava married? Is she happy?"

"What question is this?" said Anne.

Mary faced her mother. "Did Hava marry a man she chose?"

"Hava married a man chosen for her."

"Did she know him?"

"Yes, child. Hava married Samuel the sandal maker. He came here many times before we made the marriage promise."

Marta took Mary's hands into her own. "Be not troubled. He is a good man. Hava is well cared for. Samuel looks at her with the same eyes that Joachim sees Mother Anne."

"What do you see in Hava's eyes when she looks at her husband?"

Marta smiled. "Her eyes shine."

Mary was filled with relief. "Will he allow her to travel here?"

"I am certain he would. But, that you would not ask of her, for she is great with child. Her second."

"Her second?"

Anne reached for Mary. "Daughter, you pale. Do you ail?"

"I... I... did not plan for such news. When I think of Hava we are but children." Mary felt disoriented. When she dreamed of returning to her father's house, she saw it as the day she left with Joseph.

Jude waited with his wife and sons, Joses and James, at his side. When Mary saw them, she cried out. "Look at these boys! They favor their mother." She called Jesus to her side. "Here are your cousins."

Jesus went to them and kissed their cheeks. "Peace be with you." At that moment the three boys loved each other.

Joses turned to his mother. "May we show Jesus the hill?"

"Mary, shall we let the boys run?"

"Go," Mary answered, happy that Jesus was in a place where he was free to laugh and play with other children. She wanted to drop to her knees and thank the Lord God of Abraham for this blessing.

Joses and James led Jesus through Anne's garden and up the path. They stopped at the rock outcropping. Jesus looked down into the valley. He saw that it was as his mother has described. Below were the grey tops of the olive trees, further below a patch of fig trees. Oxen and donkeys grazed beside sheep in a pasture protected from the road by great cedar trees. Joachim's fields awaited planting. On the road, a donkey pulled a cart. Far down into the valley, Jesus saw the dark green circle of the threshing field and the curve where the road disappeared into the hills and climbed to Sepphoris.

Joses grew impatient. "Come, there is more to see," he pulled at Jesus' sleeve.

Jesus laughed and followed Joses as he moved upward. He asked James, "Where does the path lead?"

James, the shy one, was pleased Jesus spoke to him. "To the hill top and across the hill to a pleasant stream that trickles into a pond. It is there we go to bathe."

At the top, Jesus climbed the boulders and paused again to survey the land he now called home. He breathed in the air and whispered a prayer to his father in heaven, "Thank you, father for bringing me to my Eden."

"Come," shouted Joses, who was moving away toward the south side of the hill.

Jesus and James followed. They heard the water rise and fall when Joses jumped into the pond. Jesus looked at James and laughed. "The day is well meant for bathing, is it not?"

"So be it," answered James as he pulled his tunic over his head.

They threw their garments over the reeds at the edge of the pool. Jesus found a rock and held it high. "Let us see who can catch the rock before it falls to the bottom." He threw the rock into the pool and dove after it.

Joses came up, with the rock in his hand. "Ah, my brother, be careful so as not to lose such a valuable gem. The pool is deep. The bottom cannot be reached." He tossed the rock back into the water.

James went after it.

Joses and Jesus floated on their backs.

Joses became alarmed. "I cannot see my bother!" Joses dove and came up sputtering, "He is not there!"

"Worry not, brother," Jesus answered, turned his head and blew upon the water.

James' outstretched arm rose up out of the water, the rock in his grasp. He came up gasping.

Joses grabbed James and held him, keeping his head above the water while he caught his breath.

James pushed Joses away and dropped the rock. He watched it slide down though the water. He told them, "I followed the rock a long way. I almost lost my air and feared I had gone too far, but I was caught in an eddy that sent me upward."

Joses was bewildered. He knew of no swirling water in the pond. He looked to Jesus.

Jesus smiled, but said nothing.

Joses understood that Jesus had saved James' life. *Mother Anne's stories are true. Jesus is the Messiah for whom all have waited.* Joses marveled. *He is but a boy, like me. How can this be?*

The three pulled themselves from the pond, dried their bodies with their tunics, and dressed.

Joses quietly told Jesus, "There is a path that will take us through the olive grove. It will put us in the courtyard more quickly than returning the way we came."

"So be it," answered Jesus.

In a few minutes they stood in a courtyard full of activity. A lamb on a spit dropped fat on hot coals mixing the aroma of roasting meat with the always-present scent of cooking bread. Marta and Ester were placing small clay bowls near rugs spread on the ground in a semi circle.

Ora, wife of Jude, saw her sons and Jesus and frowned. "Why is your hair wet?"

Joses answered. "Mother we took Jesus to the pool. He is talented in the water."

It seemed an odd answer, but Ora let it pass without question, for she had much to do. "Go. Gather grass for the fire."

When the lamb had cooked, the men and boys stood upon rugs and the women stood near the fire pit. Joachim raised his hands in prayer. "Lord God of Abraham, we thank you for the many blessings you have brought upon this house. We thank you for entrusting into our care your son. Guide us in all things. Thank you for your gift of the food we are about to share."

A chorus of "Amens" followed.

Joachim remained standing as his sons and grandsons sat upon the rugs. When they were settled, he spoke to his family. "God has given back to us our daughter and has added two brothers to this house. For this we are grateful."

"Thanks be to the Lord God of Abraham," answered Joachim's family.

"My children, we know not whether the dangers that caused our dear ones to flee Judea have passed. In all ways, we must take care to protect them from the outside world."

Anne paled, her fears for her daughter and grandson returning.

Mary reached for her mother's hand. She whispered, "Worry not. Yahweh is with us."

"Ah, child, I fear it is my nature to worry. Have not the lines grown deep into my face in your absence?" She remembered how Mary had offered the child to the wild woman in the Temple. "You will take care with him, will you not?"

"Yes, mother, I will. But, we must let him be a boy as are the others."

"So be it," Anne signed, wishing she could tie Jesus to her wrist and never allow him from of her sight.

Joachim continued to direct his family. "Speak not of their presence in this house to any but who gather here today."

"So be it," came an uneasy reply.

Joses thought of what Jesus had done at the pool and that he had known to speak not of it. He understood who Jesus was. He marveled that he could be at ease in his presence.

Jesus – who sat next to Joses – turned and smiled, as if he had read his thoughts.

Sensing that a somber mood had overtaken his family, Joachim called out. "Let us be happy. Let us feast. Today is a day of joy never to be forgotten." With that he sat.

Marta carried a large bowl with pieces of lamb and roasted vegetables to Joachim. Ester followed with rounds of bread. Ora carried a pitcher of wine. They went first to Joachim, then to Jesus.

As the men and boys ate, the women gathered at the fire pit and also took of the bowl. When all had eaten, they cleared away the bowls and cups.

Darkness fell. Jude brought out a flute and began to play. The woman and children sat next to their husbands and fathers.

The night grew late. Parents carried sleeping children into the hill. The courtyard gate was closed and barred. A lone lamp sat on the ground between Joseph and Joachim.

Joseph turned to the father of his wife. "We have spoken much tonight of the lives of our families these past five years. Tell me of other things."

"What do you wish to know?"

"The Romans. Are they a threat?"

Joachim shrugged. A trace of amusement entered his voice. "They are but a small presence in Galilee. They are needed in places of far greater concern to the august Caesar than this small plot of land. To him we are fleas on the back of a stray dog. If we bite hard enough to make the dog yelp, he swats at us."

Joachim's mood darkened. "Even as we speak, a brave – perhaps foolish – coalition travels from Jerusalem to Rome to protest the harsh rule of Archelaus."

"Archelaus is like his father, then?"

A bitter laugh came from Joachim. "They say he is more debauched."

Thinking of his broken house in Jerusalem, of his neighbors' losses and of the threat to his own family, Joseph felt his anger rise. "More so than Herod? This is a concept my mind cannot receive."

"I cannot speak in fact. I have only what comes into my ears from the lips of travelers on the road beside my fields."

"This coalition? Will they be heard? Is it possible Archelaus could be removed?"

"I hear there is among them one who has amiable connections with the Roman elite. Many of our people distrust him, but they do not object to using him to find a way to air their complaints."

Joseph felt a twinge of excitement. With Archelaus gone, reclaiming his land might be less dangerous. "There is hope then?"

"Ah, my son, there is always hope. My hope is that this group of men bring no harm down upon us." Joachim shoulders sagged. "I say, let sleeping dogs lie. Rome allows us to worship in our own way. What more can we ask of a foreign ruler?"

"How does Antipas rule here in Galilee?"

"With a lighter hand than does his brother."

"There is unrest here as well?"

"In Herod's last years he became preoccupied with the building of his great burial monument in the desert south of Jerusalem. Our brethren in Sepphoris were emboldened by his lack of attention to Galilee. They claimed Sepphoris a City of the Jews; one independent of outside rule. It was a terrible decision.

"Herod called upon Rome. Caesar sent the Legate Quirinius to Herod's aid. His soldiers burned the city to the ground. We could see the smoke rising from the ruins. The few Jews they did not slay, they sent to Rome in chains."

Joachim shrugged. "Antipas as Tetrarch of Galilee has restored order. Our people have always chaffed beneath the rule of the Herodians. The unhappy are always with us, is that not so? In these days they are small in number and do not show their faces."

Joseph was stunned. Word of this slaughter had not reached the refugees in Egypt. Had he returned too soon?

Joachim saw concern on the face of Joseph. He reached over and touched Joseph's arm, his voice again serious. "My son, worry not. This is as safe as place as any. Antipas has formed a stable alliance with Quirinius. He enjoys his new palace in Sepphoris. We are merely stupid peasants to him. As long as our tax money flows into his pockets and our fields fill his table, he heeds us not.

"I am told there is much work in Sepphoris for one such as you. It is said Antipas plans to make the city his personal work of art." Joachim suddenly began to laugh. He was so amused he could barely speak. "It is said he has plans to build a theatre where he will present Greek tragedies to his ignorant Galileans."

Joachim rose taking the lamp with him. "Come, let us go to our pallets savoring this day. You have made my heart sing with joy. Thank you,

Joseph, for returning to us. We will keep your family safe here in the hill."

"So be it," Joseph answered rising from his rug. He followed Joachim to the door opening into the room prepared for him and Mary and Jesus. He remained troubled. He was not yet convinced that the sons of Herod had given up their father's quest to find the new King of the Jews.

He lay upon a rug spread on the ground next to Mary. As he drifted off to sleep, he decided to leave Mary and Jesus in the safety of the house of Joachim. He would seek work in Sepphoris, for much could be learned in such a place.

CHAPTER TWENTY: MEMORIES

Thirty-four Years After His Birth

"Laban, these were happy times for me. My precious daughter and grandson were with me. This house filled with love and laughter. Joseph found work in Sepphoris. At first he walked there daily, but as time passed he often remained in the city, returning to us only for Sabbath." Anne leaned toward Laban and whispered. "It is difficult for a man to live in the house of his wife's father. We all felt his discomfort. I am not proud of this, but I was not sorry for his absence." She shrugged. "Yet even then I harbored resentment toward him for the time lost with my daughter.

"Mary told me that Joseph shared with her gossip he heard in the marketplace. Joseph said a few in Sepphoris grumbled of being ruled by Rome, but he heard no further talk of revolt. Antipas, caught up in the rebuilding of his city, ruled there with an even hand and provided many jobs.

"Joseph told Mary he heard that things were not the same in Jerusalem. Caesar, tired of the bickering in Judea, removed Archelaus, banishing him to Gaul. The Roman General Copious was made procurator over Judea. He was as brutal as any before him. He restored order. He controlled the Temple priests. Rome was happy.

"Our people were unhappy. Copious proved also a man of greed. He grabbed Herod's lands. He increased an already heavy tax burden upon us. A bloody revolt erupted. He quelled it without mercy. Joseph told us on the surface Judea was calm, yet beneath rumblings of revolt continued. I was relieved when Joseph said it was not yet safe to reclaim his house."

Her voice trailed off, as if this next thought had not before occurred to her. "Joseph began to spend less time here in the hill."

Caught up in Anne's fascinating history lesson, Laban forgot his doubts of the validity of her story. He even forgot about Rebekah. He was surprised when laughter returned to the voice of Anne.

"Jesus brought us much joy. I loved watching him grow. He looked at everything with new eyes. I remember one day during the winter rains he was standing next to me in the upper room."

Anne turned to Laban. "Joachim moves my loom to the upper room when the rains arrive." She looked into the distance and continued, "We were standing at the window looking down into my garden. Jesus laughed and said, 'Look, Mother Anne. The puddles are jumping.'"

She grinned at Laban. "And they were. The falling rain hit the packed ground and the water pooled there rose up. I have never since watched rain without thinking of that moment.

"We could have spoiled him, but he would not allow it. When Joses and James were old enough to work the rows, Jesus insisted he labor beside them. When they went to work the threshing circle, so also did Jesus."

CHAPTER TWENTY-ONE:
THE THRESHING FLOOR

His Eighth Year

The sun was nearly at its highest point in the sky. Jesus was excited. This was his first venture away from the hill since Joseph had brought him there from Egypt.

From his pallet, he had watched his parents arguing long into the night until, at last, Joseph relented. Jesus could go with the men, but promises were required of him.

Joseph had told him, "You must walk past a serpent overrun by an ox cart, or a sparrow fallen from a tree. If you see a man with a broken arm, or sores on his skin, you must walk past. You must not reveal your gifts."

These were not promises easily made. To pass by an animal whose life had flown? It would be painful, but this he could do. To pass by a suffering man or child and turn away knowing his touch or whisper could ease suffering? This was a terrible burden. He was slow to reply. "So be it," he muttered.

Joseph was firm. "Jesus, even if there is no other person nearby, you must not do these things. Do you understand?"

"So be it," he answered, his jaw set.

"Reveal to none that you read and write, nor that you decipher numbers. Your skills exceed a grown man's and will draw attention to you."

"So be it," he had promised.

Jesus stood next to a cart fully loaded with freshly gathered sheaves and empty clay pots. Sweat trickled down the sides of his face. Joses stood next to him, grinning. "My brother, the true work is yet to come."

"So be it," Jesus answered. He took a long drink from the water bag that dangled from a rope slung around his neck.

Jesus heard Joachim's whistle. The carts began to move. He and Joses walked together, holding hands and laughing.

He found it good to walk along the road he so often watched from the rock out-cropping above Mother Anne's garden. Here the road was broad and flat and the hills to the north seemed further away. The freshly gleaned fields threw the perfume of newly disturbed earth into the air.

A rider on a fast horse swept by. A donkey cart bearing covered cargo came from behind them and trotted past, the driver pulling up on the reins to offer greetings to Joachim.

"Men on important business," Joses told Jesus.

It was not long when they pulled the carts to a stop beside the threshing floor. A track led from the road and separated the floor from a small grass-covered field where goats grazed. Beyond it, Jesus could see a series of small huts and a well.

Niv, the thresher, stood beside the road, his eldest son by his side. He greeted Joachim. "Ah, my friend, it seems the fields have been generous this year."

"It is so. The Lord God of Abraham has blessed my house."

Niv laughed. He had worked Joachim's wheat and barley crops for many years. The Lord God of Abraham seemed always to bless his fields.

The thresher's veiled wife appeared bearing water. The thresher took the gourd from her hands and offered it to Joachim. His wife stood behind him.

Joachim drank. "Your hospitality is generous as always." He turned and waved at Jacob.

Jacob pulled from the lead cart two folded mantles and carried them to Joachim. Joachim took the first and handed it to Niv. "A gift for you, my friend, made by my wife's hands."

Niv accepted the dark brown, thickly woven garment. "Many thanks. Tell your wife that she honors me."

Joachim retrieved the second mantle. The cloth was pale, not quite white, and softly woven. This too he handed to Niv. "Ah, you know my Anne. She would not allow me to bring the sheaves without a gift for your wife."

"Ah, Joachim. I will wish to marry her again when I see her in such a beautiful mantle."

The men laughed. Niv handed the two garments to his wife who turned away, glad for the veil that hid from the men her smile and the tears slipping from her eyes. She hoped that one day the Lord God of Abraham would allow her to speak to the woman who wove these beautiful cloths.

Joachim's sons and grandsons waited on the road while he and Niv came to terms for the work to be done.

As they watched the two men, Joses explained to Jesus what was to follow. "We will spread the sheaves over the floor. Niv will bring oxen and tether them so that they must circle the floor. With their great weight and sharp hoofs the oxen will separate the grain from the stalk.

"The thresher will drive them until the stalks are ground into straw. As the oxen work, we must sweep the stalks so that none are missed by the feet of the beasts."

Niv and Joachim kissed each other's faces, signaling an agreement had been made.

Jacob led the carts onto the track to the edge of the threshing floor.

Niv's son led two great beasts onto the floor. They were slow moving, grey oxen with bulging shoulders and fat hips above short legs. Jesus noted that they had wide feet and sharpened hoofs.

Jesus helped pull the wheat from the carts and spread the sheaves upon the floor. He accepted a broom from the son of Niv and stood aside as the thresher lined up the oxen.

The beasts walked one behind the other, starting at the outer rim of the circle. Guided by the prodding of the thresher's stick, the oxen moved around the circle, working their way to the center and back to its outer edge.

James, Joses and Jesus swept the sheaves. It was not hard work, but Jesus discovered the importance of moving swiftly for the hooves of the oxen discerned not boy from stalk.

They worked all afternoon. Jacob and Jude carried fresh sheaves from the carts. Joses, James and Jesus continued sweeping.

When Niv declared the grain separated, he pulled the oxen from the floor. Joses and James laid down their brooms.

Jesus was surprised and happy to see that while they worked, Niv's family had laid out rugs in shade provided by linens tied to poles. He laid down his broom and followed James and Joses from the threshing floor.

Water and cloths were ready for washing. Prayers were spoken. Veiled women clothed in silence served bread and thick broth flavored with carrots and onion.

They took their time over the meal for the winnowing could not begin until the early evening winds arrived. Jesus leaned back on his elbow. He decided the company of men was good.

When the linens overhead began to flap, Jesus saw a line of women walking toward the floor. Joses turned to him. "Our rest is over. We must help with the winnowing."

Inside the circle the sons of Joachim and Niv scooped up wheat and tossed it into the air. Grain, heavier than straw, fell to the floor, the light winds sent the straw to the side.

Joses and James collected the straw and stacked it at the circle's edge. Jesus swept the grain into piles.

When the winnowing was done, the men bundled the straw and stacked it outside the threshing floor. As they worked, women of the house of Niv carried sieves and baskets into the circle. Each squatted before a pile of grain.

Jesus was fascinated as he watched the graceful movements of the singing women working in cadence with their music. Each bent in fluid motion as one hand scooped grain and dropped it onto the sieve. The other hand shook the sieve, forcing the grain to drop through into a basket, leaving stones and tares in the sieve. With a flick of the wrist, this chaff was tossed aside and the sieve placed again over the basket to accept another handful of grain collected from the pile on the threshing floor.

Jesus, Joses and James stayed close to the women. As their baskets filled, the boys carried them to the carts and emptied them into waiting clay vessels.

When the winnowing was done, Joachim pulled a pot heavy with grain from a cart and carried it to Niv. "Many thanks to you and your family." Niv accepted the payment and the men kissed each other's faces.

Joachim's sons and grandsons filled the carts with bundled straw, hiding the precious cargo of grain. It was not until their work was finished that Jesus realized lamps had been lit around the circle and the sun had vanished from the sky.

Niv's family provided water for them to wash their faces and hands. The men and boys of both families embraced as they said their farewells. The veiled women lined the road and waved good-bye as Joachim's small caravan moved away from the threshing circle.

Joachim, seeing how weary were the young boys, insisted Jesus, Joses and James ride in the carts. Joachim walked at the head of the first cart.

Recognizing that they were heading home, the donkeys pulling the other carts required no guidance, leaving Jacob and Jude free to walk behind the last cart.

Jesus leaned back on the straw and studied the cloudless sky. Stars crowded together crossing the sky in broad bands, casting enough light upon the road that there was no need of a torch.

The canopy of the thick stand of olive trees hiding the house of Joachim from the road darkened the steep path up the hill. The men and boys were happy to find Sarah, Anne, and Mary standing along the edge of the trail bearing lamps.

Few words were exchanged as the weary men unloaded carts and stacked the bundles of hay and bags of grain in the courtyard.

Mary smiled, seeing Joseph kiss the head of the sleeping Jesus as he lifted the boy from his bed of straw and carried him into the hill.

CHAPTER TWENTY-TWO:
THE PARABLE OF THE EAGLE

His Tenth Year

The rains had not yet come. Though there was the work of mending plowshares and sharpening scythes to be done, it was a time of year easy enough to allow for the luxury of a visit to Nazareth.

It was mid-morning and few were about. The women had made their trips to the well. The men were busy at their shops. Jesus stood outside the house of the tailor. Joses was inside being measured. A woman shepherding a group of schoolboys approached.

Jesus smiled and greeted the boys. They stared at him, wondering why this boy was free from the tedium of numbers and letters and the memorization of scripture. One whispered to another, "Do you know him?"

"No," he whispered back. "He must not be of this village. Perhaps he awaits his master. Look the other way. We do not wish trouble."

"He does not seem as one to fear."

Their guardian covered her face, yet returned Jesus' greeting, "Peace also to you."

As the group passed, Joses came out. One boy poked the other with his elbow. "See, I was right. He is a servant."

"I like that boy," the other replied.

Jesus asked Joses, "Have you now clothing suited for taking a wife?"

Joses frowned. "It is done. The garments will be ready. This measuring is a nuisance. Let us move along, so that I may walk off the feel of the hands of the tailor."

Jesus laughed.

Joses had resisted being attended by the tailor. Joachim insisted he wait no longer. The family of Sarah had announced the day of her wedding. Before a second Sabbath her brothers would escort guests to the center of the village where their betrothal would be completed.

The two young men stopped to drink at the well. Jesus was certain Joses had asked him to accompany him for a reason. He was patient. Joses would reveal his purpose in his own time.

When they left the village and found the road, Joses began abruptly. "I embarrass myself in the presence of Sarah. My feet tangle in my mantle. My tongue says things my mind does not expect."

Jesus laughed. "Is this not good, Joses?"

"This feeling..." he hesitated. "Difficult is this love of a woman unlike love of a sister. This marriage would be easier if I did not feel so."

"How can that be?"

"You know that the family of Sarah is poor."

"This is no burden. The house of Joachim has no need for her to bring coin into it."

"This is so. What concerns me is the lack of such a need is why her father so readily agreed to give her as my wife."

"You wish to take her as wife, do you not?"

"Oh, yes." Joses took a deep breath, his chest rising and falling. "I fear Sarah does not feel toward me as I do her. I do not want a wife only because she has been bartered."

"They are all bartered, Joses," Jesus reminded, his voice soft.

"Yes, but have you not seen how happy my mother is with my father?"

"It is true."

"I want that for my wife as well."

"Joses, is it not true that love of woman for man comes after the betrothal? You worry needlessly. I have seen the eyes of Sarah when you approach. I see in them the same joy I see in yours when you look upon her." Jesus placed a hand on Joses shoulder and leaned close. "At this very moment she is giving thanks to the Lord God of Abraham that you have taken her. She gives thanks not for the security of the house of Joachim, but for expectation of a happy life with a good man."

Joses stopped and turned to face Jesus. "Truly, you see this?"

"Yes, Joses. Worry not. You will have a happy marriage and children who will give you much joy."

Joses laughed. He seemed a new man. "Let us celebrate. I have figs and water. Let us sit under that tree at the curve of the road. My father will not be angry if we tarry. The work is light and he is a benevolent man."

They sat in the shade of the tree, ate and greeted travelers upon the road. They heard the running horses before they saw one come around the curve. A few paces behind the first, two more riders appeared. They whipped their horses, trying to catch the one in the lead.

Neither Jesus nor Joses were alarmed at the sight. They knew these were not robbers chasing a lone traveler. The first horseman was the son of a nearby farmer who, like Joachim, owned large fields. This son, though old enough to take a wife, ran wild. Jesus and Joses assumed the chasers were servants forced into a race.

Joses was angry. "He will wear the soul out of that animal. The little horse should not be treated thus. We will find it dead in a ditch and a servant left to walk while the son of Elkanah rides another steed to its death."

"Yes. It is hard to watch this waste. The son of Elkanah does not understand what God has given him."

"If I could, I would take a whip to him," Joses told Jesus.

"If you could, would not that make you the same as the son of Elkanah?"

"Would it, my brother? Is it wrong to punish a wrong doer?"

"Joses, recall you standing with me in the fields watching the eagle teach his youngster to hunt?"

Joses was irked by this sudden change in conversation. "What? Why ask you such a thing?"

"Do you?"

"I do." Joses quieted, and thought of the warm afternoon when the barley was high and ready to be picked. They had gone with his father to assist in the harvest. He remembered standing next to Jesus. As they paused to take water, Jesus had told him to look up.

They saw an eagle, its wingspan so great it blocked the sun and cast a large shadow as it flew over them. They watched it sweep, hover and dive into the field. In an instant they heard its strong wings beat against the stalks as the bird worked to rise into the sky. He came up fast. When he was above the barley, they could see a fat mouse wriggled in his talons.

They watched the great bird soar through the sky and land in a tall tree at the edge of the fields. In seconds, a smaller bird rose out of the tree. It hovered a moment, as if unsure of its action. Then it too swept over Joses and Jesus. The young eagle circled the field several times, building up courage for an attack. When finally it spotted its prey, it wobbled rather than hovered. It fell into the field. Stalks bent and waved. They heard the sound of flailing wings as the bird labored to gain height.

Joses and Jesus laughed when the young bird rose into the sky carrying in its talons, not a fat mouse, but a shard from which fell clumps of dirt.

When the little bird returned to the tree, the great bird rose into the sky, swooped over them, fell into the field, came up with another fat mouse in its grip and flew back to the nest.

The young bird rose up again from the tree, this time with less hesitation. It flew, hovered more steadily, dove and rose, but returned to the nest with empty talons.

Joses and Jesus watched the two birds repeat these patterns until at last the young eagle rose up from the swaying stalks with a fat mouse gripped in his razor sharp talons.

Joses smiled, remembering how he and Jesus had rejoiced at the younger bird's success.

Jesus spoke. "Joses, when the small eagle failed to retrieve a mouse, did the great eagle peck out his eyes?"

"No. He was patient. He flew again and again until the small one found his mark."

"Did we not celebrate when we saw the mouse clutched beneath the breast of that young eagle?"

"Celebrate? We shouted with joy."

"Then, let us be patient like the great bird. One day we too shall shout with joy when the son of Elkanah has found his mark."

"Elkanah is a good man. Has he not come to the aid of the house of Joachim when the harvest was more than we could manage? He deserves a better son."

Gently, Jesus chastised Joses, "It is not for you to judge what one man deserves." Jesus rose. "Come, let us be on our way. I wish to reach the groves before the sun is low in the sky."

Joses gathered the remains of their meal and stuffed it into his bag. He knew Jesus was right in his thinking, but it was difficult to see such meanness go unpunished. "Few are fortunate enough to own a horse. None should mistreat one," he grumbled.

Jesus laughed at the stubborn Joses. "Elkanah is a patient man. The horse is strong. Worry not."

The walk was not long and soon they turned on to the broad path that led up to the house of Joachim.

CHAPTER TWENTY-THREE:
ENLIGHTENMENT

Thirty-four Years After His Birth

Caught up in Anne's story, Laban did not hear the garden gate latch nor did he hear the steps of Sarah. He jumped when she spoke and was unnerved by the stern expression he saw upon her face. He saw that she carried the bag containing his writing tools and the skin.

Sarah placed the bag on the ground and her hands on her hips. She stared at Laban, but addressed Anne. "Mother Anne, the sun is past its highest point in the sky. You have spoken far too long."

Anne's laugh was soft. "So I have." She turned to Laban. "Forgive me, son. You must be weary of the sound of my voice. I forget myself." She struggled to rise.

"Mother Anne, let me help you." Sarah slipped her arm around Anne and lifted her from the chair. As they left the garden, Sarah nodded toward to bag on the ground. "You are free to do as you wish."

"Thank you," Laban managed. Sarah's message was clear. He was to put words to skin. Yet, he knew he was not ready for the task. Laban decided to find the rock out-cropping upon which he had stood with Daniel. There he could think through these new stories from Mother Anne.

Laban sat with his legs dangling over the canopy. He watched a blue thrush hop from treetop to treetop. Somewhere in the dense foliage a warbler sang.

Below, men and women worked in the fields. The men cut the wheat, the women bundled it. A donkey trotted along the road pulling a cart. A clump of turbaned men in flowing robes walked toward Sepphoris. High above, in the distance, sunlight glistened on the white walls of the city.

A light breeze brushed Laban's face. His thoughts began to clear. How was it, he wondered, had Anne learned to be such an effective storyteller? She makes this Jesus seem a child wise beyond his years. By wrapping her fantasies with life's ordinary tasks, she makes her tale ring true.

Laban shrugged. Does not, he reminded himself, every woman speak overly well of the children of her children? Yet, he knew this was beyond fondness. A line from scripture came to him. "And you, Bethlehem, land of Judea, are by no means least among the rulers of Judea; since from you shall come a ruler who is to shepherd my people Israel."

He shivered, then shrugged away the thought, telling himself this child of whom she speaks may have been birthed in Bethlehem, but the preacher Jesus was known to rule no land.

He was embarrassed that he had been caught up in Anne's dreams. Inwardly, he shrugged again, reminding himself, *I have been told to write with integrity that of which she speaks, not to judge the integrity of that which she speaks.*

He set his mind to the task that lay before him. When he worked out in his head how he would record Mother Anne's story, he returned to the garden.

Before he put ink to skin, he reread that which he had already written. To these words he added:

Herod the Great heard of the birth of a new king of the Jews and commanded his soldiers to find the child. Joseph, Mary, and Jesus fled to Egypt in the arms of angels.

Upon the death of Herod, an angel spoke to Joseph in a dream commanding him to leave Egypt and return to Israel. Joseph, upon arriving in Jerusalem, decided to take his family to Galilee to live with the family of Mary in the house of Joachim in the Nazarene hills. There they kept the child safely hidden.

Laban read all that he had written. "Angels, angels, angels," he laughed. Who, he wondered, might believe such a tale?

What now? Sarah had said he was free to do as he wished. He could not explore the hill for fear of stumbling upon another private matter. The morning had passed swiftly. He had not tired. He did not wish to lie in the shade of the gate.

He remembered watching Daniel enter the grove from a place near the rock outcropping. Surely he could find the trail that led to the fields. He would go there and offer his help. Perhaps, in this way, he might repay the many kindnesses offered him by the house of Joses.

Laban placed his writing tools in the bag. He stowed it beneath Anne's chair with the skin, leaving it unrolled to dry.

He climbed up the path to the rock outcropping. Laban left the rock and worked his way down to the place where he thought Daniel had entered the grove. Within a few steps he found a narrow trail.

It was hotter in the grove than at the top of the hill. In a few moments, sweat began to drip into his eyes. He lost the trail. Rough grasses grew high and scratched his legs.

He knew as long as he moved downward, he would find the road that edged the fields and eventually find Joses and Daniel. When he found himself climbing upward, he turned around. He plunged through the trees creating his own path.

Birds began an angry sounding chatter.

"Forgive me for disturbing you. This is not pleasant for me either," Laban grumbled.

The grove was not deep but it was steep. Laban was running when he made it to the road. He was across the road and at the edge of a field before he could stop himself. Relieved to be out of the groves, Laban laughed out loud.

The wheat at the edge of the road stood high hiding the fields. Laban remembered that the field where Daniel labored was not hidden from the road. He began to fear he had a longer walk before him than he calculated.

Laban felt the earth shake. He heard a rumbling sound behind him. He did not think it the noise of wooden wheels on hard dirt. *What is happening? Is the earth splitting?*

He turned to stare at the curve in the road. It was not until he saw a flash of sunlight bounce off the tip of a spear that he realized it was the feet of soldiers he heard and felt. Many soldiers.

He heard a voice calling out the cadence of their march. Panic seized Laban. Fear froze him in place. *They have come for the people of the house of Joses. They will find the writing by my hand!*

Strong arms grabbed Laban and dragged him through the wheat standing at the edge of the road. A hand pressed hard over his mouth and nose. He was shoved to the ground.

The man fell upon him. "Speak not, move not," Daniel whispered and stared down into Laban's fear-filled eyes. He slowly released his hand from the boy's face and a put a finger to his own lips.

Laban nodded to show Daniel he understood that he must be still.

They dared not breathe as they lay in the furrow listening to the heavy footsteps of a fully uniformed soldier and the flutter of the flag tied to his spear.

Behind the flag bearer came the clatter of the hoofs of a prancing horse. The animal came so close to the wheat they smelled its breath.

Eighty soldiers marched past, footsteps thundering in the ears of the two young men hiding beside the road. The ground upon which they lay trembled.

Panic returned to Laban, filling his mind with questions. *How many are coming? Why do they come this way? Have they been to Nazareth? Is my family safe? Do they know of what I write? Do they know the truth about the house of Joses? Have they raided the house in the hill? Were they climbing up as I was climbing down? What of Rebekah?*

Suddenly, Laban was seized by anger so intense his body went rigid. He had heard the stories of what soldiers did to women after they had killed their men. How dare they come here, hunting us as if we are animals!

Daniel had to hold Laban still and frowned another warning.

Laban forced himself to lie quietly. It seemed to him that the soldiers filed by forever.

When, finally, the soldiers could no longer be heard, Laban tried to rise. Daniel held him to the ground. He whispered, "We must wait a few moments more. There may be others behind them."

Laban nodded.

Daniel released his grip and rolled onto his back away from Laban. Daniel was afraid. He silently sent prayers to Jesus asking him to keep his father safe.

Further down the road, Joses and the field workers continued to cut wheat as if there were nothing amiss. The women who had been bundling wheat hid behind the workers, lying flat behind severed stalks. The men had thrown dirt over them.

The Centurion studied the workers in the field as he led his troop of soldiers past. Peasants, he thought. Not worth the bother. His orders were to search along the Sea of Galilee where the rabble-rouser had done his preaching. There he would find enough of these odd people to please Pilate. He spat onto the road. The Sanhedrin and the Pharisees had joined forces to pressure Pilate to act against them. Fearing another uprising by these Jews, Pilate agreed. Humph, he snorted, thinking of the Procurator of Judea. "Weak," he growled aloud, speaking to himself. "One not able to govern one small city."

For the Centurion, battling an armed enemy was honorable. Routing from hiding those who would threaten Roman rule was honorable. Chasing misguided peasants was a task that filled him with disgust. He wanted it over and done. He kicked his horse into a trot. Behind him, eighty soldiers bearing heavy packs stepped up their pace.

Laban breathed shallow, quiet breaths. He heard the sweet song of a bird in the distance. He remembered his walk from Nazareth and the climb through the brush to the house of Joachim dug in the hill. *Was that only yesterday? These people are kind and good. They have made me feel as if I were one of them, as if I have known them all of my life.* Anger washed through him. *The family of Joachim brings no harm to any. Why must they be pursued?* He heard the bird song again and relaxed. The bird sang louder.

Daniel sat up, cupped his hands around his mouth and imitated the song of the bird. He turned his head and gave Laban a soft smile. "They have passed. No other soldiers come."

Laban too sat up. *A signal! The song of the bird was a signal!* He brushed grass off his arms, looked at Daniel and said, "Thank you."

The two stood. They brushed dirt and straw from their garments. Laban asked, "How is it that you knew I was on the road?"

Daniel laughed. "Ah, Laban, you do not slip through the forest on the soft pads of a leopard."

"You saw me coming through the grove?"

"I tried to warn you, but you did not understand. We make the call of an angry bird when there is danger and a sweet one when all is safe."

When Laban realized that it had not been birds disturbed by his clumsiness chastising him in the woods, his face burned. Daniel had seen him thrashing about.

Daniel spoke next. "Laban, why were you coming down the hill?"

"Mother Anne needed rest. With the sun still high in the sky, I hoped I could help in the fields."

"You are very generous." Daniel did not sound as if he thought Laban foolish.

"Daniel, have you always posted spies along the road?"

"No, Laban, we have not always done so. We must be more careful now. Many come to our door for help. More people know who we are. We fear one day a careless word will lead the Romans to our gate."

"I assure you, Daniel: your secret remains well kept in Nazareth. We have heard no one speak of Jesus living in the house of Joses." He nearly added that his father would not have sent him to them if he had known they were the family of the preacher, but stopped the words from leaving his mouth.

"Perhaps. Laban, I will take you to my father." He turned and began walking between rows of wheat stalks.

Laban felt his legs grow weak as he began to think of what might have happened on the road. How easily the sword of a soldier could have sliced through him! They would not have bothered to throw his body to the side. The soldiers would have marched over him and left him for carrion.

Laban's thoughts raced as he followed Daniel. He was surprised he could feel no anger toward this man Jesus who seemed the cause of this new danger reaching up into the Nazarene hills. The man this family thinks is the Son of God. A man he had never known. He was surprised at how much anger he now harbored toward the Romans. Men he had never known.

Laban caught up with Daniel. "Your Jesus is known to be of our village. The Romans may have been there! I must go see about my family."

Daniel kept walking. "Let us first go to my father. He will know what to do."

Walking atop the stubble between harvested rows was as difficult for Laban as was coming down the hill. Daniel seemed to flow over it. Laban worked to keep up with him. He did not mind that the difficult ground made conversation impossible. He did not wish to argue with the man who saved his life.

In a few moments they were near the gathered workers. The women, who were in the field to bundle the grain, were brushing dirt from their hair and clothes. The men were huddled around Joses, talking excitedly.

Laban heard a woman call out. "Joses, Daniel comes."

The men turned in unison toward Daniel and Laban.

Relief was clear on the face of Joses, yet he did not smile. "Laban? You bring Laban?" Joses asked as the two young men came up to them.

"I found him on the road," Daniel explained.

Laban's words fell out in a rush. "He saved me. Forgive me for adding to your troubles. I only meant to be of help to you." He looked down, feeling as though he spoke as a child caught stealing a fig from a tree.

"Ah, yes. Well, this is good, is it not?" said Joses. The other men nodded agreement. Joses smiled. "You look as if it were a difficult walk here. Was it not?"

"It was enlightening." Laban answered, ignoring Joses' effort to lighten the moment.

"Enlightening, you say? In what way?"

"Well, I have learned why birds call and sing in the woods." Laban did not laugh when he said it. It was not a joke to him. He continued, his voice urgent, "I must ask to be released of my obligation here for a short while. I must return to my village to see that my family has not come to harm. I will return to complete the task assigned."

"We are through here in the fields today. Let us all go up the hill. Perhaps a messenger will come to us with news from Nazareth."

"Sir, I thank you. I need to see for myself."

Joses could see that Laban was determined to go home. "At least let us give you a clean garment and a donkey to ride. The Romans think all followers of The Way are the poorest of the poor. A man in a clean tunic on a donkey trotting down the tract will not be one with whom they will bother."

"So be it," answered Laban, thinking that a donkey would make it possible for him to be home before nightfall.

"Daniel, collect Asia Three for Laban," Joses said as he pulled his own tunic over his head.

Before Laban could protest, Ezra had stripped him of his torn and dirty tunic. Joses brushed dirt and wheat from Laban's hair and helped him put on the garment he had pulled from his own body.

Daniel returned with a donkey. "The birds tell us the danger has passed and the road is safe. The soldiers passed by the house in the hill."

Joses turned to the others. "All is well." He turned back to Laban, helping him onto the donkey's back. He placed the end of the rope tied around the donkey's neck into Laban's hand. As he handed Laban a stick, Joses looked directly into Laban's eyes. "Yahweh is with you," he said.

"I will not tarry in Nazareth if I find my family well. Peace be with you."

"Peace be with you," answered Joses as he slapped the donkey's rear.

Asia Three jumped and trotted off. Laban turned away from the men, using the stick to hurry the animal.

Laban entered the village of Nazareth as the sun fell behind the hills. The streets were quiet. The houses shuttered. Nothing seemed amiss. When he reached his house, he found the lower floor closed and the gate locked. He could see candlelight shining from the windows in the room above the shop. He banged on the gate and called out. "Father, it is I."

His sisters popped their heads out a window. "Laban," they cried. "Mama, Papa, it is Laban!"

Quickly his parents and sisters were at the gate, welcoming him as though he had been away many days. His mother and sisters kissed his face. His father closed the gate and tied Asia Three to a post.

Laban discovered grain in the pack thrown around the neck of the animal. He allowed his sisters to feed and water the animal.

When Asia Three was tended, Laban and his family climbed the ladder to the second floor. His father closed up the house behind them.

They sat in a circle on the floor. His mother placed a large platter of food before them. They ate and began to pepper Laban with questions. They were surprised by his speedy return and eager to hear of his visit to the house of Joachim.

His father begin their inquiry, "Laban, how is that you return so finely dressed and with an animal such as this?"

Clearly nothing had transpired to threaten his family. Laban decided not to speak with any but his father of the fears that had brought him rushing home. *There is no reason to worry them needlessly,* he told himself.

"The master of the house of Joses insisted I borrow the donkey. She has an odd name. They call her Asia Three. It seems they have a tradition of naming animals in succession." He blurted his next words, "My work there is not yet finished. I must return to the house of Joses tomorrow."

The family of Laban was puzzled. His father spoke, "My son, we are happy to see you and have missed your presence among us, despite an absence of only a short while. Yet it troubles me that you have found this sudden need to return to us, with a plan to leave again just as suddenly."

Laban silently debated. *If I tell my family of the dangers to the house of Joses, will he allow me to return? If I speak of such things, how can I keep secret these are the people of Jesus?* "Father, may we speak of this later?"

Surprised, yet understanding that Laban had a private matter to discuss with him, the potter agreed. "So be it." For the moment he would delay relieving his curiosity. "So, son, what stories bring you from the countryside?"

"Yes, Laban," his sisters and mother joined in. "We wish to know all that you have seen."

He tried to answer their questions, swearing by the Lord of Abraham that the fields of Joses were grander than any they could imagine.

There were many questions he could not answer. "How many were in the household?" asked his mother, thinking of the cooking that must be done for such a family.

"This is hard for me to answer. They call each other, of all ages, brother and sister, all except one, the widow of Joachim. She is very old and every member of the house speaks of her and to her as Mother Anne."

Afraid of hurting the feelings of his own mother, he did not tell them that he too called Anne "Mother." "They come and go, and different women serve meals, and work in the fields."

"Are they rich?" asked his older sister.

Laban's chest heaved and he frowned as he thought of how to answer. Finally he said, "I do not know. The house of Joses is rich in land, yet they live a simple life. The women do not wear jewelry, nor fancy combs in their hair. Yet all have plenty to eat and they are generous to all outsiders."

"What is this tale you have been asked to put upon skin?" asked his mother.

"It is long story, not yet written and I have promised not to reveal it."

"Not even to your own family?" His mother was offended.

"Do not ask this of our son," said the father of Laban. "This tale is precious to this family. We must not abuse their trust in Laban."

They questioned Laban until he threw up his hands. "I tire. I wish to fall upon my pallet," he begged.

As soon as he made the request his mother insisted the family bid him good night. In a few minutes, all lay upon their pallets. She put out the candle and the house was quiet.

In the morning before the sun brought light, while his mother and sisters were still sleeping, Laban and his father readied Asia Three for the return journey to the house of Joses.

The father of Laban spoke softly, "My son, you have caused me to lose much sleep, for my mind was busy with this puzzle. If your task was not complete, what brought you home in new clothes on a borrowed animal?"

Surprised at the words that fell from his lips, Laban answered, "Father, I have met a woman in the house of Joses to whom I wish to be betrothed."

"Have you?"

"Yes. Her name is Rebekah. She is very smart and very kind, as well as beautiful."

"Does she know of your intentions?"

"I think not. I have not spoken to anyone of her."

"Then what makes you think she favors you?"

"I am not certain that she does. I am certain her family would not allow her to marry one she did not favor. I can think of no other way to find out than to ask for her."

"Let us be cautious in this. Do not speak of marriage in my absence. Agreed?"

Laban hesitated, but he was an obedient son. Finally, he answered,

"Yes, Father."

"When your task is complete and you return to us, we will talk. Should we decide such a proposal should be made, I will go with you to the house of Joses."

"Then I have all the more reason to return quickly. I do not wish to tarry with this decision. She is of age. One such as she may have many men asking for her."

The potter could see his son was disappointed that he had not readily agreed to this proposal. "Laban, despite your age, you seemed just a boy when you left, but now I see a man standing before me. Know that I received your request with solemnity."

"Thank you, Father."

"Go. Complete your work for them. May the God of Abraham watch over you. Peace be with you, son."

"And also with you." Laban mounted the donkey, looked down at his father and asked, "Father, do you believe in angels?"

"Yes, son."

"Have you seen one?"

"No."

"How, then can you believe in them?"

"Why, son, have you not read of them in scripture?"

"Yes."

"What more do you need?"

"I am unsure. Peace be with you, father." Laban urged the donkey forward. He left the house of his father and the village without looking back.

His father watched Laban until he was out of sight. He was surprised at how melancholy he felt. *What,* he wondered, *meant this talk of angels? What of these new clothes? A wife! What will his mother think of this?*

Asia Three, sensing she was on her way home, needed neither rein nor stick to urge her on. Laban gave her head and used the time to think of the fair Rebekah. *She cares for me. I know it. But, they are all kind in that household. Perhaps she is only being a gracious host? No, there is a look in her eyes, I have not seen from any other woman. I am certain she feels for me as I do toward her. I must find a way to obtain a marriage promise. I will find a way to obtain the marriage promise.*

Laban dismounted when he reached the place where he should leave the road. Asia Three balked at being pulled through the brush and Laban had to grab the animal's head and pull her onto the faint trail. He pulled hard on the lead as Laban picked his way up the hill. When the path broadened, Asia Three shook her head and ceased to resist.

When Laban neared the clearing, he heard singing. He recognized it as the "forgiving" prayer. He heard the singing voices of men as well as women. He carefully entered the clearing to avoid exciting the goats and hens.

He was standing at the opening in the courtyard wall when Daniel saw him. As soon as the prayer was over, Daniel stood and called out, "Welcome, brother Laban. Thank God you have safely returned to us."

Laban smiled, happy to be greeted so. "Peace be upon this household," he answered. A chorus of like greetings came to him from the people in the courtyard.

Daniel directed a boy to deal with Asia Three, and Joses waved Laban inside.

The courtyard was full of people. They sat in a circle, men and women together. Children played behind them. He recognized several field workers, and saw others there who were unknown to him.

When he reached Daniel and Joses, they embraced him, kissed his face and made a place for him to sit.

Joses stood and spoke to all. "Who would like to speak of our Lord Jesus?"

A man stood. Laban was astonished. This was a man from his village. He was Amos, the bread maker; his wife sat next to him with their newborn son. He, a follower of what they say is "The Way?" Who else might I know among these people of this new way?

"I," Amos said, "was in the synagogue in Nazareth the day Jesus read from the scroll of the prophet Isaiah. He read that the Lord would anoint one to help the poor, free the unjustly enslaved, heal the sick and give sight to the blind. All who congregated there were touched by his gentle way and spoke highly of him.

"Yet when he told them that he was the anointed one of which the scripture spoke, many turned against him. These claimed Jesus blasphemed. When Jesus warned them it was they who blasphemed, the men grew angry and shook their fists at him. Others, not knowing what had transpired, grew excited.

"A mob formed. They tried to chase him over a cliff, but he walked through them untouched.

"I followed him and heard him turn to a disciple and speak with sadness that the people of his own village were blind to him. I was not blind. I saw and heard. I believed."

Laban remembered a day there was much agitation at the synagogue. His father had hurried his family away to their house. He closed the gate and shuttered the windows. Clearly his father felt it was not safe to be in the crowd, yet he did not explain these actions to Laban. Perhaps this was the day of which this man spoke?

A woman stood. "When my husband was alive, he fished the Sea of Galilee. We were there when Jesus fed the people. I stood close to him and I swear to you I saw Jesus take from a boy a basket holding only five barley loaves and two fish. Jesus handed over the basket to those who traveled with him. I watched them walk among the crowd. From that small basket all were fed and yet there was food remaining! I swear by the Lord, God of Abraham, this is the truth. Even I ate of the bread from that basket."

Another woman stood. "I was with Mary, mother of Jesus, at a wedding in Cana before he began to preach," she said. "During the celebration the wine was used up. The bride was dear to Mary. To save the family from embarrassment, she asked our Lord to help. He had only to say the word and the water became fine wine. I was shocked. May the Lord God of Abraham forgive me, I thought he was a magician. I did not know yet who he truly was. I swear to you this did happen."

A man rose. Laban had never seen one appear so full of joy. "I was a leper. Now I am not. All I did was ask and he healed me. He sent me to the Temple to show the priests that I was forgiven. Though he bid me speak to none of how this came to be, I could not refrain from shouting his blessed name to any who would listen. Jesus did not punish me for disobeying him." He held out his arms and pulled pack the sleeves of his tunic.

"As you see, I remain clean."

The man next to him stood. "What he says is true. This man is my brother. When he was unclean I left him food, but always I had to walk away from him. That day as I was turning away we saw Jesus approach. I saw Jesus touch my brother. I saw the sores fall from his skin. My brother speaks the truth. He was unclean and Jesus made him clean."

Laban had heard Jesus called a healer, but never before had he heard it from one he had healed. Could it be that Mother Anne's stories be truth? Was this family the most blessed?

Several more spoke of seeing Jesus heal the sick and give sight to the blind. Others repeated stories of Jesus' miracles of which they had heard, but not witnessed. A man claimed he had seen Jesus bring a dead man to life.

Just as he was beginning to believe this crowd came this impossible declaration. A dead man brought back to life? He knew such a thing could not be.

He was certain these good people believed that of which they speak. Laban sighed. He wished he had known this man Jesus. He longed to know how the preacher had cast a spell upon so many.

Late in the afternoon, Joses rose and thanked those who shared what they knew of Jesus. He motioned to his wife, Sarah, to bring a loaf of bread and to his son Daniel to carry to him a bowl of wine.

Joses lifted the bread high in the air and spoke, "This is Jesus, the bread of life which comes down from heaven and gives everlasting life to the world. Whoever eats this bread will live forever."

Laban watched as the bread was passed around, each person in turn tearing a piece from the loaf. Laban was frightened. He did not wish to insult his host by rejecting food, yet he was unsure of the meaning of this ceremony. He wished he could ask Joses to repeat the prayer. *Surely,* he decided, *I did not hear clearly. Surely he did not say the bread is Jesus?*

He had no need of fear. Although the bread was passed among all who sat around him, it did not come to his hand.

Joses lifted the bowl of wine. "This wine is the blood of our savior Jesus Christ, shed for us so that we may be acceptable to God, the Father. Drink this in memory of him." This too reached every hand but that of Laban.

The women began to carry food from the fire and all who were there ate and rejoiced in the presence of God. Laban ate with them.

Though he sat in the midst of the crowd, Laban felt alone. *All of these people truly believe in the man of this family. How can so many be fooled?* He envied their joy. *If only an angel with great wings the color of the sun would come to me, then I too could believe.*

Lost in his thoughts, Laban did not notice the visitors to the house of Joses leave the courtyard. The gate was closed and the lamp stands taken away when Laban woke from his musing and rose to climb the stairs to the upper room. There he found Daniel already sleeping.

Laban woke before Daniel. He found lying next to his pallet his old tunic. It had been mended and freshly washed. He dressed and was one of the first in the courtyard. In a few minutes the ritual of breaking fast began. As soon as the final prayer had been spoken, Laban entered the garden.

Anne was sitting in the garden, waiting for Laban before the sun rose. She was anxious for him to come to her. She grew weaker each day. She longed for her final sleep. She has glad when she saw him come through the gate.

"Peace be with you, Laban," she said.

Laban grinned. He knew not why, but he was very happy to be there.

He felt as if he always had sat at her feet. "And also with you, Mother. Are you well today? Have you more words to put upon skin?"

"Indeed, Laban, indeed." Anne settled back against the curve of the carved cedar trunk. *The boy is a good listener. James has chosen well.* She began speaking immediately. "Jesus was nearly a man when Joseph took him and Mary away. It filled me with sadness."

CHAPTER TWENTY-FOUR: PASSOVER

His Twelfth Year

The house of Joachim was happy. The day of travel to Jerusalem had arrived. Packed carts lined the steep path that led to the road below.

Preparing for the feast had started weeks in advance. The women sewed new garments to be worn in Jerusalem. Sleeping rugs were mended. A small cloth purse was sewn and filled with coins for each person. Extra grain was milled and figs dried. Jugs were filled with olive oil. Flat rounds of unleavened bread were baked and stacked in the upper room until the day of departure. A tent was pulled from storage deep in the hill and checked for damage and mended.

On the final day, their best wines were poured into clay vessels. Water bags were filled at the well.

A few were chosen to stay behind to watch over the house and animals in the fields, so that marauders and bandits could not take advantage the family's absence. Those who stayed would travel to Jerusalem the following month for the second Passover, as all Jews were required to make the annual pilgrimage.

For this Passover, Jude – father of Joses and James – was chosen to remain behind with his family to protect the house of Joachim.

By the time the sun filled the sky with light, Jesus and Joses were standing atop the hill. They could see dust billowing on the road, stirred by the feet of many travelers arriving to join the caravan of the house of Joachim. It was not for safety that these families wished to travel together. It was for the joy of their company.

The families would walk together, the men leading animals pulling the heavily laden carts. They would sing psalms together. The men would speak of crops. The women would tell of the feats of their children. The young men would gather at the end of the caravan and exchange harmless taunts.

"I will miss your company, Joses."

"And I yours. The second Passover is never as exciting the first. Though the merchants are glad of our coins, they are weary of crowds and send us quickly on our way. Even the Temple priests seem tired of greeting pilgrims."

"Yes, this is so. I shall save my coins for you, so that you will have extra to spend in Jerusalem. You will light up the eyes of even the most bored peddler!"

Joses laughed. "Such sacrifice is not needed, Jesus. Keep your coins. Perhaps you will find one more in need of them than I."

"So be it," said Jesus.

Jesus embraced Joses, kissing both sides of his face. "Peace be with you."

"And also with you," Joses replied.

Jesus turned and walked down the hill. He found his mother on the path.

"Where have you been, my son?" she asked when he came up to her. "I've been looking for you."

"What may I do for you, dear mother?" he asked.

"Go and find my husband. Ask of him what is needed."

Walking past three tightly packed carts, Jesus found Joseph standing with Joachim not far from the road.

"May I be of help?" Jesus asked Joseph.

"Yes. Your brothers gather. You will walk together at the end of the caravan to see that no child is lost. If anyone is hurt, I will send for you and you will heal them in secret. Be careful on the road, son."

"So be it." Jesus replied. He looked forward to being with the other young men of this family and of other families joining them as they moved along the road. He loved the long walk to Jerusalem, but he looked forward most to his reunion with his beloved cousin, John.

Obeying Joseph, Jesus again climbed the hill and entered the clearing. Jacob, Marta, and Joses' younger brother James stood at the edge of the clearing. Joses stood near the courtyard opening, his arm around his wife Sarah.

Though Joses longed to be in Jerusalem with his best friend, the others in the clearing did not object to being left behind. The work would be lighter during the festival week, and when the time came for the second Passover, the city would be less crowded and easier for them to pass through the streets.

The wheels of the carts began to turn. Jesus hugged and kissed those who would stay. Laughing, he pulled away from them and turned toward the path. "Peace be with you," he called back.

"And also with you," they responded with such sincerity they seemed to sing the words.

Jesus joined his cousin John, the son of Jude, and Ezra and Eyal, sons of David, at the end of the line of those moving down the path. In a few minutes, all were on the road and heading south.

At the place where the road crossed the trail through the hills to the village of Nazareth, Hava and her family waited. Joachim greeted her husband Samuel into the caravan.

Mary and Hava danced in each other's embrace and held each other, laughing and talking as they rejoined the line of travelers. Joseph held onto the hands of Hava's small daughters and laughed as they babbled and squealed in the excitement of being on the road.

It was a journey of three days. The Passover pilgrims stopped midday, rested and ate a cold meal. Afterwards, they moved along the road until they were mere shadows in the night.

They slept rolled in rugs, saving the tent for use just outside the walls of the city on the cleared land reclaimed by Joseph.

Elizabeth and John traveled with neighbors to Jerusalem from En Karem. Arriving before the family of Joachim, John raised their small tent inside the wall surrounding the place where the house of Joseph once stood. Consumed by excitement, John awaited the arrival of Jesus.

When Zechariah died, John had become even more withdrawn. Though he was an obedient son, as soon as his daily tasks were completed, he left his mother to run through the hills surrounding their village. He seemed not to care for the company of people.

Elizabeth laughed as she watched her son run along the street, studying the travelers entering the city. *The one he loves comes soon to this place. It is good to see him happy.*

She did not worry for the safety of her son among these crowds. Thousands of Jews were in the city for Passover celebration. The Romans and gentiles were far outnumbered. For this week, Elizabeth believed, the city truly once again belonged to the people of Abraham.

On the morning of the first day of Passover week, the city was within the sight of the family of Joachim. The closer they were to the northern gate, the slower their progress. On the road below, large crowds of people waited to enter the city.

Jesus raced to Joseph, who walked with Joachim at the head of their caravan. "I wish to go before you and find my cousin John. He waits anxiously for me at this moment. It is hard for him. May I leave you so that his fears will be allayed?"

Joseph was pleased to see Jesus exhilarated by the hope of soon seeing his cousin. He considered the request. He knew Jesus could easily find the place. "Go," he laughed.

Jesus raced down the hill.

Joseph and Joachim watched Jesus wriggle through groups of travelers until he disappeared in the mass of people, carts and animals at the city gate.

Jesus easily slipped through the crowd and found the path that ran through the garden area beside the most northern city wall. He laughed, seeing that John stood at a crossways, studying all who passed. He called out, "Peace be with you, cousin."

John turned toward the sound of Jesus' voice. When he saw Jesus, he jumped and laughed. He ran to him, grabbed him and kissed his face. His voice was jubilant. "I have long waited for this moment, my brother! Let us go to my mother, who awaits your mother with as great expectation as I have waited for you!"

The heart of Elizabeth sang seeing the two boys together. She wished her son could always be in the company of Jesus. For it was only then did she see John's restlessness put aside and that he seemed truly happy.

"Peace be with you," Jesus called to her.

Elizabeth opened her arms and embraced Jesus. Laughing, she answered, "And also to you my dear one." She grasped his hands and stepped away. "My, how you have grown since last Passover! You are now taller than my John!" See looked past him. "Your mother – where is your mother? She comes, does she not?"

Jesus released her hands. "Yes, it will not be long and this space will overflow with the household of Joachim."

"Come, follow me. We have set our tent on Joseph's ground. We can wait their arrival there. I have honey cakes."

Together they sat upon rugs in the shade of the small tent, sharing Elizabeth's fine treats and stories of En Karem. In this way they passed the time until Joachim led his family out of the crowds.

Mary, who ran ahead of her husband, was the first to greet Elizabeth. Their reunion was quick, for the carts were behind her. It mattered not. Simply to see each other was all that they needed to feel as if they had never parted.

Declining food and drink offered by Elizabeth, the family of Joachim immediately set to work. The carts were unpacked. A fire pit was dug. Men pounded tent poles into the ground and raised a tent made up of three separate rooms.

Jars of olive oil, grain, wine and stacks of unleavened bread lined the edges of the tent. Mary and Anne found the baskets containing special platters, plates, bowls and cups and carried them into the center room of the tent.

Small rugs were piled on the ground. Rugs for sleeping were rolled and placed inside the rooms of the tent. In the middle and largest room, Joseph began to build a long low table around which the family would sit for the Passover meal.

When the encampment was in order, Joachim announced that those who wished could enter the city. To fulfill the requirement that a second tax be spent in Jerusalem, he gave each who left for the city a small purse holding coins. With this money, they were allowed to purchase doves to be sacrificed from vendors lining the western wall of the Temple and trinkets for themselves from other merchants.

The women – Anne, Mary, Hava, and Elizabeth – chose to rest rather than enter the city and soon were napping on pallets within the tent set up by Elizabeth and John.

Jesus and John entered the city together.

Jesus had barely passed through the gate when he stopped, stilled by the entrancing mixture of fragrances swirling around him. A perfumed woman walked by, a hint of exotic Babylon trailing behind her. A baker passed with a basket of fresh breads on his shoulder, filling the air with mouth-watering aroma. Exotic fruits on display before merchants' booths sent their subtle scents upward.

John nudged Jesus forward. As they walked, all around they heard a pleasing combination of voices. Men, arguing in the western accents of people from the Plane of Sharon, stood in a group before a vendor of leather goods. At another table, they heard bartering in the rough talk of men from Galilee. Jesus stepped aside for a cluster of elegantly-robed men who heeded no others on the street as they debated in the sophisticated speech of the Sadducees and the haughty voices of the Pharisees.

Jesus came upon a beggar and gave him a coin. Seeing this, many beggars in the street crowded around him, jabbed the air with their arms and shouted for alms.

He raised his hand and the ragged men grew quiet. Though his purse was small, Jesus placed a coin in each outstretched hand. When he pulled the lining out of the bag to show that he had no more to give, the beggars backed away and let him pass.

He found John standing before a woman in tattered clothing. Her uncovered hair, tangled and filthy, fell over her face as she stretched out her thin arms for mercy. To her, John gave all his coins.

She rose to thank John, but when she saw Jesus, her face hardened. "You are the son of the carpenter Joseph."

He could see that her eyes were not those of a mad woman, but those of one who had known much sorrow. "How is it that you know me?" he asked.

"I held you in my arms when you were but a babe. The house of my husband sat close to the house of Joseph before the soldiers came and tore both apart."

"How is that we find you here in this condition?" Jesus asked.

"Joseph warned us in the middle of the night. He told us to take away the babies. We did not believe him. That same week we were overrun by soldiers returning from their crimes Bethlehem." Tears streaked her face.

Jesus wept with her.

John stood, mouth agape. Looking at one to the other, saying nothing.

The woman swayed as she spoke, remembering the awful night. "The soldiers were covered in the blood of murdered children. They behaved as drunkards. It seemed a game to them as they swept through our small lane.

"They ran a sword through my husband as he stood before our gate. With my children, I ran up the hill to hide in the gardens. Three soldiers chased me. They did not care that I had a girl child as well as a boy. They killed them both. They shared me and left me for dead.

"I would that I had been. I returned to the house of my father, but he cast me out. God will not let me die, so I am as you see me here."

"God has given you many sacrifices. Come with me. My mother will help you." Jesus took her hand and began to lead her. "You will suffer no more," he promised.

Jesus took the woman to a public well and helped her wash her face and hands. John had disappeared but reappeared at the well with a pair of sandals in his hands. He washed her feet and helped her tie the sandals.

Jesus again took her hand and began to lead her through the crowds. As they walked, John pulled a piece of flat bread from his pocket and gave it to her.

She ate, taking small bites and chewing slowly, for she had learned not to eat quickly when she had gone days without food. For if she rushed to quell her pangs of hunger, the little that got into her stomach would fly back out of her mouth. After three bites, she found a pocket in her ragged mantle and slipped the remaining bread into it.

In minutes they were at the large tent spread out near the very ground upon which her house once stood. She cried out and sobbed when she saw the place.

Mary stood in the shade of the tent flap. When she saw Jesus and John with the horribly dirty and thin woman her mouth fell open. "What is this?" she asked.

"Mother," Jesus began, "you know this woman. She has suffered much because of me. I have brought her to you."

"Where did you find her? How is that I know her?" Mary reached out to take the hand of frail woman.

Rachel backed away and pointed at Mary, her long dirty nail curving like a scythe. "I am Rachel. You were my neighbor until you brought evil upon us. Emmanuel," she snarled. "I knew no good could come from giving a child the name of God. You have blasphemed." She spat in Mary's face.

"Rachel!" Mary backed away in fright, wiping her face with her sleeve.

Jesus gently laid his hands upon the head of the poor woman and said, "Demon of hate, leave this woman. I command you."

Rachael bent over and gagged. From her mouth a gleaming black serpent as long as she was tall fell to the ground and burst into flames. A sudden wind swept the fire upward where it became a thin, black cloud flying over the city.

Rachael fell into a faint. Jesus caught her and held her in his arms. He carried her into the tent like a father carrying a sleeping child to her pallet.

"Mother, when she wakes she will be a new woman. She will remember her losses, but her pain will be healed. She will know that her children rest in the warm embrace of my father in heaven."

John came with a clay jug filled with water. Elizabeth was with him, carrying a bundle of clean cloths.

Mary waved away Jesus and John. "We will take care of her. You have done well to bring her to us. Now leave us."

The next morning, Jesus signaled John to walk with him. When they were out of the tent, Jesus announced, "I go now to the Temple."

"So be it. So shall I," John answered.

They walked eastward along a path beside the northernmost wall. The path turned to the south and within a few steps they passed the Eastern Gate, continuing on until they found the southern end of the Temple Mount where they entered the baths to be cleansed. Afterwards, they climbed the steps leading to the triple Huldah Gates.

Paying no heed to the golden doors and glistening marble walls, Jesus walked directly to the Court of the Priests, where long lines of men waited with doves in cages and bleating lambs slung over the shoulders. Others led cattle into the court. He and John found a place to squat against a wall, unnoticed in the throng of pilgrims.

The boys watched as priests took animals to the slaughtering place, where blood from the slashed throats of lambs and cattle poured into gutters leading down into vats. They saw priests transfer bloodless carcasses to a skinning room.

Jesus knew the blood would be sold to farmers in the Kiddron Valley to be used to nourish the soil. He knew the hides would be sold to tanners in the city. It was a profitable business. The money from these sales went into the Temple treasure, from which the High Priest was generously paid.

They watched the skinned animals being thrown upon a huge pyre sitting before the most sacred place in the Temple, the Holy of Holies. Acrid smoke rose to the sky and the stench of burning meat filled their nostrils.

A man and his servants walked past John and Jesus. This man, dressed in flowing robes and a gold-trimmed mantle, with great show ordered his servants to bring an ox to the table.

Jesus thought of Rachel and the beggars roaming the city and his heart hurt. *How many could be fed with the grain grown in the furrows dug with the strength of this great animal? What good is this burning, but to line the pockets of the High Priest? My father has no need of this. They abuse his house.*

Jesus' heart also ached for those who came with virtuous motive and for whom great sacrifices were required to present a simple dove to the fires. He rose and walked away from the blood letting.

John followed. They walked from the Court of Priests, through the Court of Israel to the Nicanor Gate and through it into the Court of Women, from which they could step into the outer court, the Court of Gentiles.

Jesus found a place to stand to watch the intense activity. Jews from around the world stood in lines at tables where sat moneychangers who – at great profit – traded Temple Tyres for coins from many countries.

Vendors carrying cages of doves or leading crying lambs wound through the crowds, selling the animals. Here, Jesus did not find the strange mix of voices pleasing. Rather, their harsh and noisy bartering burned in his ears.

John studied the parapet above the Temple walls, where Roman soldiers stood watching the huge crowds move in waves in and out of the courtyards. Though the Romans could not enter the Temple, they worked with the Levite Temple Guards. One signal from above and quick action was taken. The slightest disturbance was met with severe punishment. With thousands of Jews in the city, the Roman Procurator greatly feared an uprising. His soldiers were vigilant.

John did not like being on the Temple grounds. It did not feel sacred to him. Standing atop a hill, feeling the strength of winter rains upon his face was sacred to him. He longed to be in his small village, exploring the caves in the hillsides behind the house he shared with his mother. Were it not for his precious cousin, never would he place a sandal in this filthy place. "Let us leave this place," John whispered to Jesus.

"So be it," Jesus answered.

Jesus led John from the Court of Gentiles into the street, away from the Temple, past the market and out of the city through the northern gate. In a few moments, they welcomed the freshness of their encampment and the familiar aroma of food upon the fire.

The family of Joachim – as did most Jews visiting the city that week – spent the holidays leading up to the Passover supper free of labor and in the company of family and friends, many of whom were seen only at this time.

Together they made forays into the city, first to the Temple to make their sacrifices, and then to admire the architectural splendor commissioned by Herod The Great. Seated on the highest point in the city, the Temple's marble walls rose into the sky, gleaming white as the purest clouds. Sunlight caused blinding shards of light to shoot into the air from the heavy layers of gold encrusted on the ornate designs around and upon the doorways. Not even the most devout Jew could disagree that, in this, Herod had indeed outdone Solomon.

Jacob and his son John guarded the women of the house of Joachim as they made their one trip inside the city. There they ran their hands along the silks and pointed at gold and silver jewelry. Anne found an ivory comb. Mary purchased an ivory needle for her mother. Hava found colored pebbles for her daughters, who she had left in the care of Elizabeth.

Each day throngs of people moved in waves throughout the city.

Vendors hawked. Musicians strummed lyres in the streets. Behind the vendors, down alleyways, beyond the eyes of the crowds, dice rolled and women sold their services.

The night before the day of the Passover meal, Adi and Adah – daughters of Hava – swept the tent with great drama, in search of unleavened bread. When they found none, they went to Joachim and showed him their empty baskets.

Joachim spoke, "All leaven that is in my possession, that which I have seen and that which I have not seen, be it null, be it accounted as the dust of the earth."

With this proclamation, the house of Joachim gladly found their rugs for the night.

In the early morning of the day of the Passover meal, the women of the house of Joachim unwrapped the dishes and utensils to be used for the special meal. At each place, Mary and Rachael put a small plate and four cups. Rugs were lined on the floor surrounding the table. A platter of bitter herbs and a bowl of vinegar were put before the place of Joachim.

Anne ordered vessels of wine be placed in the middle room near a stack of unleavened bread loaves. Olive oil lamps were placed on lamp stands at the corners of the table.

When the preparations were complete, Mary and Elizabeth left visiting the city to the others. They were content to sit inside the tent of John and Elizabeth taking advantage of the opportunity to talk of their sons and lives. Rachael, feeling safe, lay upon a rug and slept.

"Are you well?" Mary asked of Elizabeth.

"My bones ache, but I still have my sight and hearing. For one with as many years as I, I am well."

"And, John, is he of great help to you?"

"As much as he can be. But there has always been a way about him that disturbs his days. He cannot sit still, except to eat." She laughed, "He gobbles his food as if I were about to grab it away." She saw concern flash across Mary's face. "Do not worry for me, dearest sister. I hear God calling."

"Oh, please, Elizabeth, do not speak so. I cannot imagine a life without you."

"Mary, be ready. You know I have lived much longer than most women." Elizabeth dropped her head. "I do worry for John. He will be an orphan soon. My neighbors promised to care for the boy, but I doubt he will let them."

"Oh, Elizabeth, send for me when you feel that your time nears. I will bring John home with me. We will keep him safe. Better still, Elizabeth, come to Nazareth with us now. Joseph can take a cart to En Karem. He will pack your goods and carry them for you."

"Let me think on it."

As Mary studied the lined face of her aged cousin she knew her Elizabeth would not return with her to the house of Joachim.

Elizabeth spoke, "You wear a dour face, Mary. It does not become you." She laughed, "Mary, I long to join my husband. Do not feel badly for me."

"Oh, cousin," she answered, "it is for myself that I mourn. But let us speak no more of such things." For now, she decided, I will enjoy the company of my dear Elizabeth and the pleasure of working beside her.

"So be it," replied Elizabeth.

As the sun fell from the sky, Joachim lit the lamps around the table as his family gathered outside the large tent.

With cloths in their hands and bowls of water at their feet, Jesus and John stood before the tent flap leading into the middle room. They washed the feet of all who came to dine. Then John washed the feet of Jesus and Jesus washed the feet of John.

Anne led each person to a place at the table first to last.

The first was Joachim. The last was Jesus who sat at the right hand of Joachim. For this meal, the men and women and children sat together. Rachael and Mary brought to each small bowls of water for hand washing.

When the hand washing was completed, Joachim rose from his seat. Though the years were wearing upon him, this day Joachim stood straight as a young man. For many years he had repeated the Passover ritual and it filled him with joy to once again stand before his family.

Joachim prayed, "Blessed are you, Lord God of Abraham, king of the universe, who has created the fruit of the vine. You, God of Abraham, have given us festival days for joy, the feast of the unleavened bread, the time of our deliverance in remembrance of the departure from Egypt. Blessed are you, Lord God of Abraham, who has kept us alive, sustained us, and enabled us to enjoy this season."

When Joachim paused, Mary and Rachel left the table and stood next to the vessels of wine. Joachim began to recite from scripture the words of the Lord spoken to Moses.

"Therefore, say to the Israelites: I am the Lord. I will free you from the forced labor of the Egyptians and will deliver you from their slavery. I will rescue you by my outstretched arm and with mighty acts of judgment. I will take you as my own people, and you shall have your God."

The women poured wine into the first cup at each place at the table. When they returned to their own places, Joachim raised his cup high and drank from it. All at the table drank with him.

Joachim pulled to the edge of the table the platter upon which bitter herbs lay. These he dipped into vinegar. He took a portion, tore it into two pieces, giving one to Jesus.

Jesus and Joachim ate of the bitter herb. Then Joachim passed the platter and the bowl of vinegar so that all around the table could partake of the bitter herbs. All took a serving of the herb, tasted it and then put what remained of their servings on the plates before them.

When the platter returned to Joachim, Anne and Elizabeth removed the cups from which all had drunk. Rachel poured wine into the second cup before each place at the table.

Adah, Hava's child, asked, "Why is this night different from all other nights? On all other nights we eat leavened or unleavened bread, but this night only unleavened bread."

Hava prompted her daughter Adi to ask a second question. "On all other nights we eat all kinds of herbs, but this night only bitter herbs. Why do we dip the herbs twice?"

Adah added, "On all others nights we eat meat roasted, stewed, or boiled, but on this night why only roasted meat?"

Joachim took a deep breath. It was time to repeat the history of the Jews. He had grown to love the telling of it and it came from his lips as if he had walked each step along the way.

"My family, listen." He paused, waiting for all to turn their faces to him, then continued. "God appeared to Abraham while he was in Mesopotamia and said to him, 'Take your family and go where I show you.'

"Obeying God, Abraham left the land of the Chaldeans and made his house in Haran. After his father died, Abraham came here to Judea, which at that time was known as Canaan. The Lord God brought him here with nothing; not one lot, not one field, not even a hut in a field!"

Joachim paused, bent slightly, looked at each person sitting at the table, smiled and whispered as if revealing a private secret. "Abraham was old and had no children. Yet, God promised he would give the land to his descendants!"

Joachim shrugged and extended his hands out palms up, yielding to the trouble that lay ahead. "God warned Abraham that before this was to happen his descendants would be strangers in a another land. A land where they would be oppressed and enslaved."

He dropped his hands to his side. With a strong voice he added, "Yet, so that his chosen people would worship him, the Lord God of Abraham promised to bring judgment upon those who enslaved his people."

Anne smiled at Mary and leaned back on her pillow. Her expression reminded her daughter that this was a story that would take long in the telling. Both women relaxed, enjoying the rest the ritual gave them.

Rachael, lost from this sacred ritual for many years, sat rigid, eyes wide.

Next to each other, Jesus and John sat cross-legged on rugs. John struggled to remain still. Jesus, who leaned back with his eyes closed, placed his hand upon the shoulder of his cousin, passing his peace into him.

Joachim smiled and continued. "The Lord gave Abraham the covenant of circumcision and he gave him a son whom he named Issac." Instantly his expression sobered as he announced, "Issac fathered Jacob and Jacob fathered twelve sons."

Joachim shook his head in dismay. With a weary voice, he told them, "Eleven brothers became jealous of the one called Joseph." Joachim leaned forward and spoke as if he could not believe his own words. "They sold Joseph into slavery and he was taken to Egypt!"

The old man swept his arms out over the table. Great joy returned to his voice. "God was with Joseph. Not only did God rescue Joseph, he opened the eyes of the Egyptian Pharaoh to Joseph's great wisdom. The Pharaoh put Joseph in charge of his household and all of Egypt!"

The voice of Joachim switched to a wail. He cringed. "A great famine came to the lands." Joachim beat his fists against his temples. "Our people suffered greatly." He bent his head and was silent.

Joachim raised his head and looked into the eyes of his own son Jacob. "When Jacob, the father of Joseph, learned that there was food in Egypt, he sent his other sons there. But Joseph did not reveal himself to them. They came home with nothing.

"Jacob sent them again." Joachim lifted his shoulders and from his mouth he expelled his breath as if a great danger had passed. His voice lightened, "Joseph relented and made himself known to his brothers and made his brothers known to the Pharaoh."

Again, joy filled the voice of Joachim. "Good son that he was, Joseph did not seek retribution for the evil done to him by his brothers. Rather, he brought his father and his whole family – seventy-five in all – to Egypt, where they lived and multiplied."

Joachim bowed his head. He was silent long enough to make Anne wonder if he had lost his place in the telling of the story.

John, whose attention easily strayed, started to rise, thinking the story was done. Jesus laughed and pulled him back down to his rug.

Joachim frowned, his voice grave. "A later Pharaoh, who knew not of the power of Joseph, oppressed our people. He forced them to give up their infants! This the mother of Moses could not do. She put her tiny son in a basket and placed him into the river.

"A royal servant found the babe and took him to the daughter of the Pharaoh who brought him up as her own. Moses was educated in all the words of the Egyptians and he, like Joseph, became a powerful man.

"At forty years of life, Moses sought out his own people and offered them aid." Joachim shook his head, widened his eyes and shrugged as if he shocked by what he would next say. "They rejected him! They chased him away! Having turned away from the Egyptians, Moses had no choice but to flee. He settled his family in the land of Midian."

Joachim smiled and his voice grew strong as he announced, "At eighty years of life, in the desert near Mount Sinai, an angel appeared to Moses as a burning bush. From it Moses heard God speaking. 'I am the God of your fathers, the God of Abraham, of Isaac and of Jacob. Remove the sandals from your feet, for the place where you stand is holy ground. I have witnessed the affliction of my people in Egypt and have heard their groaning, and I have come down to rescue them. Come now, I will send you to Egypt.'

"Moses returned to Egypt, where he accomplished great deeds. He parted the Red Sea, making for our people a way out of Egypt. When they had safely passed, he made the great sea flow over the Pharaoh's soldiers.

"He led us into the desert. When we grew hungry and fearful of starving, the Lord God made quail come into the camp and rained bread down from the heavens. We called this bread manna.

"When we thirsted, God gave Moses a staff and told him to strike it upon a rock. Water flowed from it.

"The Lord God of Abraham took Moses to the top of Mount Sinai and gave him the laws by which we live. These he brought down to our people."

Joachim paused and gestured to all around the table to rise and praise God by singing words written by King David:

Praise the Lord. Praise servants of the Lord. Praise the name of the Lord. Let the name of the Lord be praised both now and forevermore. From the rising of the sun to the place where it sets, the name of the Lord is to be praised.

Lord is exalted over all the nations, his glory above the heavens. Who is like the Lord our God, the one who sits enthroned on high? Who stoops down to look on the heavens and the earth?

He raises the poor from the dust and lifts the needy from the ash heap. He seats them with princes, with the princes of their people. He settles the barren woman in her home as a happy mother of children. Praise the Lord.

Joachim raised the second cup in the air, closed his eyes and prayed, "Blessed are you, Lord our God, king of the universe, who has created the fruit of the vine." He placed the cup upon this table without drinking from it.

Joachim opened his eyes, slowly looking at all standing around the table. With solemn voice he said, "This is the word of the Lord. 'Therefore, say to the Israelites, I am the Lord. I will free you from the forced labor of the Egyptians and will deliver you from their slavery. I will rescue you by my outstretched arm and with mighty acts of judgment.'"

Again the family of Joachim sang a song of David. When the singing finished, Joachim announced. "Now let us enjoy the fruit of our labor." He motioned for all to be seated.

Anne and Rachel brought small loaves of unleavened bread and dishes of vinegar, placing them before each person. Mary carried a large platter of carved lamb and roasted vegetables. She placed it before Joachim.

The women washed their hands and then carried bowls of fresh water and clean cloths to each at the table for a second washing of hands.

When this was completed, Joachim picked up the small loaf of unleavened bread set before him and prayed.

"Blessed are you, Lord our God, king of the universe, who brings forth bread from the earth. Blessed are you, Lord our God, king of the universe, who has sanctified us with your commandments and commanded us to eat unleavened bread."

From the plate before Jesus, Joachim took a piece of bread and wrapped it around a bitter herb. He took the hand of Jesus and together they dipped the bread and herb in vinegar. Joachim placed this bread upon the plate before Jesus.

Jesus then tore a piece of bread and a bitter herb from the plate before John. Together they dipped these in vinegar and returned it to John's plate. Thus, each in turn at the table acted. When all were served in this way, they ate of the bitter herb.

Joachim pulled the large platter to the edge of the table. He served a helping of lamb and vegetables to Jesus and pushed the platter next to

Jesus. Jesus served a helping to John, who in turn served the child next to him. The platter was passed around the table until all had been served.

Joachim stood, raised the second cup of wine, and drank from it. All at the table sipped from their cups. Joachim sat and, with a wave of the hand, signaled that is was time to enjoy the meal.

With food came conversation and laughter. The roasted lamb and vegetables were a welcome treat. They ate slowly, savoring the food and the break in the formal portions of the Passover rite.

Joachim silently talked to the Lord God of Abraham as his eyes swept around the table. *Thank you Yahweh, I am blessed. You have given me many years with my family. Before me sit my sons and the sons of my sons. At my right sits your son. Thank you for entrusting him into my care.*

Joachim's eyes rested on the face of his wife. He saw that she was speaking softly to Elizabeth. *Elizabeth! What a miracle is this woman! Look at the fine son she has brought into the world. John and Jesus, they think they are men. They are only boys. Please dear Lord, have mercy on them.*

Rachael sat between Elizabeth and Mary. Many years had passed since she had sung the Psalms. She was surprised that the words came so easily from her lips. She studied the face of Jesus and wondered. *How is it that this one, not quite a man, has so much power over others? How is it that I can sit here and not hate him? If it were not for that one, might not I be living still a few steps from here in the house of my husband? Might my children be sitting at my table, singing Psalms? Yet I cannot hate him. He has brought me back to life. I was dead and he has raised me up. Please dear Lord God of Abraham, allow me to be the servant of Mary so that I might remain in the presence of her son.*

John had finished the small portions he had taken from the platter. He sat, spinning his empty wine cup as if it were a toy. *If my mother were not here, I would leave this place. This tent is confining and I long to be in the night air. I am tired of sitting. What care I that my ancestors walked the desert? What care I of these songs? The past is over. A new day comes.*

Anne turned to Joachim. Speaking softly, she said, "All have eaten. If it is your wish, Mary and I shall remove the dishes."

"So be it," answered Joachim.

Anne rose. Mary saw her rise and also stood. Rachael and Elizabeth joined them. The table was quickly cleared of all but two cups and bread at each place. Mary and Rachael went around the table pouring wine into the third cup.

Joachim stood. He broke apart the bit of unleavened bread he had saved. Each person at the table did the same with their own portions of bread.

Joachim prayed, "Blessed are you, Lord our God, king of the universe, who brings forth bread from the earth. Blessed are you, Lord our God, king of the universe, who has sanctified us with your commandments and commanded us to eat unleavened bread."

The family of Joachim ate the last of the unleavened bread. Together they stood and prayed aloud, "The name of the Lord be blessed from now until eternity. Let us bless him of whose gifts we have partaken: blessed be our God of whose gifts we have partaken and by whose goodness we exist."

Joachim added, "Blessed are you, Lord our God, king of the universe, who has created the fruit of the vine. You who have said, 'I will redeem you with an outstretched arm and with great judgments.'"

Jesus rose from his place. Though Joachim was surprised, He said nothing. He sat, motioning with both hands for the others also to stay at the table.

Mary and Rachael stood behind the table, expecting to pour more wine. Jesus gestured that they also should be seated. They looked at Joachim. He nodded that they should do as Jesus said. They too sat at the table.

Jesus began to speak, "These are the Laws given to Moses: You shall have no other gods before me. You shall not worship idols. You shall not call upon the Lord for your own vanity. You shall keep holy the Sabbath day. You shall honor your father and mother. You shall not kill. You shall not commit adultery. You shall not steal. You shall not bear false witness against your neighbor. You shall not desire the possessions of others."

Jesus paused. His eyes swept the room. He continued, "This also is the law of our Lord: As the prophets before you, you are blessed. Though you may be poor and meek, you are blessed. Though you may mourn, you are blessed. Though you may hunger, you are blessed. Though you may be reviled and persecuted, you are blessed. My father has a place for you in his kingdom in heaven. You are the children of God."

Silence overtook the family of Joachim. *Why,* they wondered, *did Jesus speak in this way?* They waited in the hope Jesus would say more but he sat, leaving them to their own thoughts.

Rachael was the only one among them who understood. *Because of Jesus,* she thought, *I mourned. I was poor, meek and hungry. Because of Jesus, now I am blessed. My heart has healed. I am clean. My spirit has been redeemed.*

Mary rose and asked Rachel to help her. Each taking a clay vessel of wine, they added to the third cup placed before each person at the table.

They set the wine pitchers on the floor and returned to their seats.

Joachim rose and blessed the last of the unleavened bread, his voice quiet. "Blessed are you, Lord our God, king of the universe, who brings forth bread from the earth. Blessed are you, Lord our God, king of the universe, who has sanctified us with your commandments and commanded us to eat unleavened bread."

When the unleavened bread was eaten, all prayed aloud. "The name of the Lord be blessed from now until eternity. Let us bless him of whose gifts we have partaken, and by whose goodness we exist. Blessed are you, Lord our God, king of the universe, who has created the fruit of the vine, who has kept us alive, sustained us and enabled us to enjoy this season."

Joachim stretched his arms out over the table, "I, the Lord God of Abraham, will redeem you with an outstretched arm and with great judgments."

They drank from the third cup.

Mary and Rachel rose and removed the second and third cups. Then they poured wine into the forth cup.

Together the family of Joachim prayed over this final cup. "Blessed are you, Lord our God, king of the universe, who has created the fruit of the vine, who has kept us alive, sustained us and enabled us to enjoy this season."

Joachim shouted, "I, the Lord God of Abraham, will take you as my people, and I will be your God. You shall know that I am the Lord, your God, who brought you out from under the burdens of the Egyptians."

His family drank of the wine, joined hands around the table and sang another song of David. When they finished, Joachim said, "Peace be with you."

"And also with you," all responded and the supper was ended.

As the family left the table, a chorus of thanks rang out to Joachim for his lively history lesson and to the women of the house who served the meal.

Hava and Rachael cleared away the last of the cups and plates.

John was the first to leave the tent. Though the wind carried on it the smell of many fire pits burning around them, the night air was cool and refreshing. Jesus joined him, standing silently beside him.

Soon all the men were gathered outside the tent continuing lively conversations. Though they spoke of their visits to the city with enthusiasm, there was not one among them who did not long to be standing upon the outcropping of rocks above the house of Joachim.

The lamp-stands in the middle room were doused and the house of Joachim rested for the night.

Long before the sun rose, Jesus woke with an undeniable urge to return to the Temple. Waking no one, he crept from the tent and slipped along the northern wall beneath the Fortress of Antonia. He turned south with the wall and found a small gate leading into Solomon's Portico.

There he found the Gate Beautiful shut tight. He sat, leaning against the portico wall, watching the black sky turn grey, then violet, then misty pink as the sun worked to rise above the distant hills.

As the first ribbon of light streaked across the Kidron Valley, the magnificent gate swung open. Jesus rose and stood before the opening. Inside the Temple, he saw priests sweeping and scrubbing the marble tiled floors and walls. Gone were the long lines of men and animals and the altar stench. *They put my father's house in order,* he thought. A calm came over him.

A shofar sounded. Jesus watched the priests abandon their tools and enter deeper into the Temple. A soft chant began. Jesus dropped to his knees and became lost in prayer.

John also woke early in the grey light of dawn. Upon seeing an empty pallet where Jesus had slept, he left the tent in search of Jesus. He was not to be found among the carts and tethered animals, nor did John find him upon the lane. John too followed the wall and made the turn south. He entered Solomon's Portico and peered through the Eastern Gate. He saw Jesus kneeling in prayer. Wishing not to disturb him, John found a place in the shadows of the wall and waited.

The priests returned, saw the boy, and worked around him. A trickle of worshipers drifted through.

As the sun rose higher in the sky, the great city heaved with waves of pilgrims pouring from every gate.

Joachim directed the dismantling of the tent. Anne made certain that the carts were packed carefully, that water bags were filled and that baskets of bread were tied to the backs of the donkeys.

Mary was not sorry to leave Jerusalem, yet she grieved over leaving Elizabeth. They embraced and kissed and held onto each other. "Come with us, cousin," Mary begged.

Elizabeth pulled away, held Mary's face in her hands and with a sad smile said good-bye. "My dear one. Worry not. Yahweh is with us always." She handed Mary over to Joseph. They heard Joachim's whistle. Elizabeth whispered, "Go, Joseph. The carts move."

Within seconds, Joachim's caravan was caught up in the eddy of people, carts and animals flowing up into the hills. Mary, caught up in her sorrow, did not know that Jesus was not among them.

In the Temple, Jesus did not stir from his prayer until a chattering cluster of schoolboys arrived for morning lessons. The sound of their Rabbi hushing them aroused Jesus. He smiled at the sight of the boys arranging themselves in a semi-circle before the Rabbi.

The Rabbi motioned, inviting Jesus into the group.

Jesus went to him and sat at the Rabbi's feet.

John stood away from the group, watching and listening.

"My sons," began the Rabbi, "you have seen here in this holy place animals being offered up to the Lord God of Abraham, is this not so?"

Heads bobbed in agreement.

"Only yesterday, did you not hear the story of our great Moses and how the Lord God of Abraham spoke to him of many things?"

Heads again bobbed in agreement.

"Among these things, the Lord God of Abraham spoke to Moses of the need for his people to repent of sin and to show this repentance through offerings. And through Moses, the Lord God of Abraham gave us laws concerning these offerings. He said to Moses, 'When any of you present an offering of cattle to the Lord, he shall choose his offering from the herd or from the flock.'"

Jesus raised his eyes to look directly into the face of the Rabbi. He spoke. "It is written, if his offering is a burnt offering from the herd, he shall make his offering a male without blemish. If his offering for a burnt offering is from the flock of sheep or of goats, he shall make his offering a male without blemish."

"Excellent, my son. You have studied well." The Rabbi was impressed. He wanted to hear more from this young one. He asked, "What other offerings may one make?"

"It is written, if his offering to the Lord is a burnt offering of birds, he shall choose his offering from turtledoves or pigeons. When a person presents an offering of meal to the Lord, his offering shall be of choice flour. He shall pour oil upon it, and dust it with frankincense. The priest shall scoop out the best part and this token portion he shall burn at the altar. No meal offering shall be made with leaven or honey. Every offering of meal must be seasoned with salt. If you bring a meal offering of first fruits you shall bring new ears parched with fire, grits of the fresh grain. To these you shall add oil and frankincense."

The Rabbi was silent as he studied Jesus. He is quick and precise with his answers. Whose student is this? And why have I not heard of him? Forgetting the others, he quizzed Jesus further, "When are such sacrifices required?"

"It is written, an offering is made when a person without intention breaks one of the Lord's commandments and realizes that he has sinned."

"Do all men offer up identical sacrifices?"

"It is written, an anointed holy man shall offer for the sin of which he is guilty a bull of the herd that is without blemish. If all of God's people err, the congregation shall offer up a bull of the herd that is without blemish. If a chieftain incurs guilt unwittingly and recognizes his guilt, he shall bring as his offering a male goat without blemish. If any member of the populace unwittingly incurs guilt and he realizes his guilt, he shall bring a female goat without blemish."

John watched as the Rabbi continued to question Jesus. He noticed that priests who had been working nearby gathered around the circle of students. He edged closer so that he could hear the whispering among the priests. Fear rose in his chest when he heard one order a student to leave and return with a priest of a higher rank. John worked around the circle until he stood close to where Jesus sat.

Seeing that his audience grew, the Rabbi decided to continue to test the boy before him. "Are there times when a man cannot offer up his guilt?"

"It is written, a sacrifice may not be offered by one who has touched an unclean thing, or if he keeps secret knowledge of a sin committed by another." Jesus paused, then added. "I say that the Lord forgives any, clean or unclean, who acknowledge to him a sin which they themselves have committed."

The Priests gasped at the words coming from the mouth of the boy and murmured to each other, "Does this boy dare interpret scripture?"

The startled Rabbi asked Jesus, "What say you?"

Jesus replied. "You need only ask and you shall be forgiven."

Seeing a priest gesture to a Temple Guard, John stepped between the Rabbi and Jesus. "Cousin, come. It is time to leave."

A commotion began at the gate. All turned at the sound of flapping sandals hitting the marble floor. They saw a man and woman running toward them, their tunics flying in the air about them.

The woman called out, "My son, my son. At last we have found you."

Jesus rose when he saw that it was his mother and Joseph who interrupted.

When Mary reached him she cried out, "My son, why have you done this to us? We have been searching for you with great anxiety."

"Why look you for me? Know you not that I must be in my father's house? That I am about my father's business?"

Mary was shocked by the sound of anger in the voice of her son. Her mouth fell open and she shuddered.

Others standing around Jesus were appalled that the boy would speak in such a way to his mother. None moved nor spoke.

John saw that a priest of high rank approached, accompanied by a Temple guard. He grabbed Jesus and pulled him from the group. Without loosening his grip, he whispered into the ear of Jesus, "Run!"

Jesus shrugged off John's grasp, turned his back upon the gathered crowd and walked away.

John, Mary and Joseph followed him out of the Temple.

No one gave chase.

CHAPTER TWENTY-FIVE:
A BLESSING ON THE HOUSE OF JOSES

Thirty-four Years After His Birth

Laban's jaw dropped. What pictures she paints!

Anne sighed. "I often told Mary she was too liberal with the boy. When I learned what had happened, I am afraid I spoke harshly to my daughter for allowing him to roam away from her eyes.

"I was shocked when she told me how he spoke to her in the Temple, for I had never heard him raise his voice in anger, and then to speak so to his mother?" Anne voice trailed off as she shook her head. "Imagine, Laban, he actually chastised her for her anxiety!"

Anne shook her head again as if she could not yet believe her own words. "I tell you, at the time, for such insolence, I would have taken a switch to him, no matter his age." She laughed at herself and muttered, "Such an old fool." She became serious and a note of sadness entered her voice. "When they brought him back, I heard Joseph and Joachim speaking long into the night. The next day they told us what was decided. I well remember his words. Joseph said that by speaking with the priests in the Temple Jesus had 'chosen the day and time.'"

Anne shifted in her chair, uncomfortable with her memories. "At the time, I knew not his meaning. As I was not given a say in this matter, I could not question him.

"Joseph said we were no longer to hide Jesus. He said he did not yet think it yet safe to return to his plot of land outside the northern wall of Jerusalem. He would find a house in Nazareth."

She leaned over and whispered as if she were about to blaspheme, "I believe Joseph sought a house of his own more than he sought the safety of Jesus. We treated Joseph with respect, but I fear in this house he was lost in the shadows of Joachim and Jesus. The boy had given him an excuse to leave the hill and he took it without hesitation.

"Mary and I wept at another separation. We saw no need for such a move. Our only solace was that Nazareth was a short journey of less than half a day." Anne fell silent.

Laban waited. He had grown accustomed to her pauses and abrupt starts, but it saddened him that Anne seemed to struggle to regain her composure. He was shocked when he realized it was not tears she sought to overcome, but anger.

Anne straightened in her chair, took a deep breath. "In the beginning, Jesus frequently came and sat with me here in the garden. I am sorry to tell you that as time passed, his visits grew farther apart.

"My daughter told me that each year he grew more quiet than the last. She told me he spent long periods praying in their garden. When Joseph died, Jesus took up his tools, but Mary said that his heart and mind were not with the wood beneath his fingers."

A melancholy overcame Anne. Her voice but a whisper, she said, "My daughter and Jesus knew of the terrible death that awaited him. Yet, in kindness, they spared me this knowledge.

"Well I remember the day when Mary came to me weeping. 'Mother,' she said, 'Jesus grows more distant and speaks of his time being short. I knew it was to come, but my heart aches. I am not ready for this burden.' Even then, I did not understand what was to come.

"We began to hear rumors about the son of Elizabeth. It was said he was even more unruly than when he was a child. Thanks be to God, his mother did not live to hear her child spoken of as a wild man dressed in animal skins! Jesus began to preach. Mary traveled with him."

Suddenly Anne realized her story had been told. Surprised to feel sorrow that her time with Laban had come to an end, she spoke with resignation. "As to his preaching, I have only the stories of others to repeat. My task here is done. Laban, go write upon the skin." She rose from the cedar chair.

Laban jumped up to help her. *Over? The story is over?* He felt a surge of disappointment.

Anne leaned against Laban. As they walked to the gate, she instructed him, "When you have finished putting ink to skin, give what you have written to Joses." She stopped before reaching the gate, lifted her head and kissed the face of Laban. "Thank you, Laban. You have been kind and patient with an old woman. God will bless you in many ways. Thank your father for sending you to us."

Words stuck in the throat of the scholar.

Sarah came through the gate. "Ah, Mother Anne. I thought I should come for you. Let me take you inside for a rest." Without waiting for an answer she put her arm around Anne. "Thank you Laban, I can walk with Mother now."

Laban released Anne.

When they reached the gate, Anne made Sarah stop. The tiny white-haired woman turned back to the scholar. "Laban, do not think these things of which I have spoken are the exaggerations of an overly doting grandmother. I swear by the Lord, God of Abraham, all these things truly occurred." She stared at Laban, then added, "Peace be with you, dear one."

"And also with you," he answered watching the gate shut before him.

Laban sat for a long time in the garden, thinking on all that he had heard that day. *Mother Anne tells this story as truth. Can there have been a man such as the one of which these people speak?* He wished he had known Jesus. He wanted to know how had he enchanted so many people.

Laban gave up trying to make sense of what he had heard. He decided to finish his work. He entered the courtyard and climbed the steps to the upper room. He pulled out the skin and read what he had written. He sighed and reminded himself: *I have promised to write with integrity all that Mother Anne has spoken. I am not required to vouch for the truth of her words.*

He stretched out on the floor to compose his final sentences and fell asleep. When he woke, the sky was dark. No noise rose from the courtyard. Laban was not offended that he had been left alone in the upper room. He was certain Mother Anne had told her family to leave him to his task.

A bowl of cold barley soup and a round of bread sat on the floor next to a lighted lamp. When he had wiped the bowl clean and eaten the last bite of bread, he began to write:

During the Passover festival in Jerusalem, when the boy was twelve years of age, Jesus made known to the Temple priests his great knowledge of Scripture. From that time until the days of his preaching, he lived quietly in the village of Nazareth.

Despite his nap, Laban felt drowsy. He pulled a rug around him. *In the morning,* he decided, *I will take the skin to Joses.*

He realized he had not seen – nor thought of – Rebekah since his return to the house of Joachim. He wondered if he would see her again before he returned to the house of his own father. He feared he would not.

He drifted off to sleep wishing Anne's storytelling had not ended. In the night he had a dream that would never leave him.

Laban saw himself standing at the square opening in the courtyard wall, watching a crowd of singing people seated in a circle atop a thin, silver cloud. The words of the beautiful forgiving prayer rose out of their mouths and flew into the air to swirl around him, wrapping him in a sweet embrace.

The dream changed. He stood at the edge of the circle, his feet hidden by the cloud. Daniel rose and made a place for him next to Joses.

People around them began repeating the stories of Mother Anne. Though all spoke at once, each voice was distinct to his ear.

He found himself looking down from the sky. He and Joses sat in the courtyard. He saw a basket of bread come to his hand. He saw that he took from the basket a loaf and tore off a piece and ate. He watched as a wooden cup came to his hand. From it he drank wine and was filled.

He was alone in the courtyard, with the preacher of whom all had spoken. Jesus embraced him, kissing both sides of his face. "Peace be with you," Jesus whispered as he passed through Laban.

Laban jolted awake. He stared into the dark, full of wonder. *I felt him. He came to me! He walked through me!*

Laban closed his eyes, savoring the warmth flowing through his body. Behind his eyelids, a soft white mist formed with a brilliant light at its edges.

Laban yearned to enter the mist, but shapeless shadows formed and re-formed, blocking his way. The mist grew brighter and took the shape of an arch.

Laban found himself behind the arch, as if standing inside a cave looking out at the day. Light swirled and filled the archway. A tiny speck of brilliant light forming in the center of the opening made Laban gasp.

His eyes flew open.

The room was dark.

He felt as if he were floating above the floor. Laban smiled. *Peace,* he thought. *This is the feeling of peace. Before this night, this word meant nothing to me, only part of a common greeting sliding easily from my lips. Now, this word fills me. I am where I should be.*

He slept again, dreaming not.

The first light woke Laban. The dream was so fresh that for a moment he thought he was still in it. Never had he known such happiness. He took a deep breath and slowly let it out.

Daniel lay behind Laban, wrapped in his rug and not yet awake. With care to be quiet, Laban stepped over him.

He picked up the goatskin spread out the night before to allow the ink to dry. Slowly he rolled the skin into a scroll and then held it against his face.

Soon he would present the scroll to Joses. He prayed he had done well and that by so doing he honored the house of Joses as well as the house of his father. Yet, he did not want to give away the scroll.

It came to him he had one more task. He unrolled the skin and stretched it on the floor. He pulled brush and ink from his bag. Beneath the words he had written, he added to the story.

As he waited for the ink to dry, Laban read again all that he had written. He feared he had read the story aloud, for at that moment Daniel sat up.

"Ah, Laban. Working so early?" he asked as he stretched, yawned, and ran his fingers though his hair.

"It is not work that I do, Daniel. This task spread out before me is a gift to me from the family of Joses. I am grateful to you."

"It is, Laban. That it is," he agreed. He rolled up his rug and placed it in the corner. Laban seemed different in Daniel's eyes. "Did you sleep well?" he asked.

Laban grinned. "I slept and dreamt so well, I am a new man."

"My brother, let us go below to break our fast. Perhaps you can tell me of this dream?"

"Thank you, Daniel. Do not let me keep you from your meal. I wish to wait until these last words dry. Then I shall come downstairs. When you see your father, please tell him that I have completed the task given to me and I will bring the skin to him."

"So be it," said Daniel. He turned and jumped down the stairs.

Laban walked to the window and looked out beyond the courtyard, over Anne's garden, beyond the tops of the olive trees and at the morning light reflecting on the far-away hillsides.

Thoughts tumbled in his head. *When this task was given to me, I wished it to be completed quickly. Yesterday I was sorry that wish had been granted. Today I feel not that I have come to an ending. I have reached a great beginning.*

Will my family understand? I fear not. How can I explain such a thing to those who have not experienced it? If I speak of this dream, my mother will weep and my sisters will stare and think I have gone mad.

Even these dark thoughts could not dampen his spirit.

He decided to leave the skin to dry and join the others in the courtyard.

Joses was the first to greet him. He grinned, grabbed Laban and kissed his face. "And so, Laban, did you sleep well?"

"I slept and dreamt so well that I am a new man. And you?"

Joses laughed, "I always sleep well. It is the field that ensures it. My son tells me you have completed your task. Is this so?"

"Yes. The ink is still wet, but the words are written."

"This is good. Let us now eat. The men wait to tend to the fields." Joses turned away from Laban and thanked the Lord God of Abraham for the many blessings upon his house.

The men made a quick meal of the barley soup and flatbreads. When they had eaten, all prayed again. In a few minutes, the workers left the courtyard. The women gathered in the open lower room and ate of the bread and broth.

Laban was not certain, but he thought during the meal some of the women whispered to each other and turned their eyes to him. He did not know that a smile had not left his face since he had descended the stairs. Their behavior bothered him not. He raced up the steps, hoping to find the ink dry.

The skin was ready. Laban rolled and tied the scroll. He stowed his brush and ink, grabbed his bag and returned to the courtyard. He carried the goatskin in the crook of his arm, as a woman carries her infant child.

Laban found Joses at the well speaking with Daniel. He waited in silence, surprised that he felt nervous. When Joses turned to Laban he announced, "I give you the story as told to me by Mother Anne. It is my greatest desire that I have been true to her tale."

"Thank you Laban," answered Joses. "I will take your words and read them to Mother Anne. We will soon know if your greatest desire has been granted."

Laban was so nervous he did not hear the smile in voice of Joses. He worried. *What if Mother Anne does not approve? Will they let me try again? Will they cast me out? No, this family is too kind. They will thank me and let me leave and they will bring another to write her words. My family will be shamed!* Fear squeezed his heart as he watched Joses enter the garden.

Daniel approached Laban. "Laban," he whispered, "let us go sit near the gate. There we will be out of the way of the women." He grinned. He too wanted to hear the words Laban had written. They squatted near the gate, ignoring the women working nearby, who also strained to hear.

Joses found Anne in her usual place, the peach colored shawl wrapped around her shoulders. She listened carefully as he read aloud her story as written by Laban. "Dear Joses, would you read it to me again?" she asked.

"Yes, Mother Anne."

The heart of Laban beat loudly in his ears. He strained to hear Joses. The writing read better than he expected.

When Joses completed the second reading, Anne considered what she had heard. *All is there, yet much remains untold. Where is the love and where is the pain? Where are we, his family?*

She sighed. Skin and ink is precious. Scholars are taught to be prudent with their tools. The boy writes well. She whispered to Joses that she was pleased with the accuracy of the writing.

Knowing that Laban and Daniel stood by the gate, Joses turned his head and said, "My sons, come into the garden."

Laban and Daniel jumped up and were quickly through the gate.

"Peace be with you, Mother," Laban greeted the old woman.

"Ah, Laban," she answered, "thank you for your beautiful words."

She approves! His heart sang. Delight showed in all their faces. Anne rose from her place and the four laughed, embraced, and swayed as if dancing.

Tears glistened in the eyes of Anne. Her breath shortened. She put a stop to the odd ballet. When she regained her breath she returned to the chair.

Joses rolled the skin, tied it, and handed it to Laban.

Anne motioned for Laban to come to her. She pointed to the ground beside her chair. There sat a lidded, olive-shaped jar with yellow flowers and green stems painted on the sides. "Laban," she instructed, "place the skin into the jar and cover it. Give it to Joses."

He did as she asked, feeling as if he held a great treasure.

Joses took the vase. "I will seal it and put it with the bones of Joachim and Joseph," he said and left the garden.

Laban was shocked. *They bury the story?*

Anne saw his distress and explained, "Laban, your words will be uncovered when the time is right. We are grateful for your work. You may be proud of it."

"So be it," he answered. *It is good,* he decided. *They protect the writing and the house of Joses. This is as it should be.*

Anne waved her hands, shooing Daniel and Laban out of the garden. "You have things to do," she told them. "Laban, your family awaits you. Return to us when you can. I enjoy your company."

"Thank you. Your invitation is kind and I hope to be here often." Laban blushed, suddenly thinking of Rebekah.

Anne and Daniel exchanged glances and smiled.

"Peace be with you, Laban." Anne leaned her back against the side of the carved cedar trunk and closed her eyes.

"Peace also to you, Mother Anne." Laban followed the Daniel through the gate.

Anne realized that at last she felt at peace. With the story told, she was free to join Joachim and her precious grandson.

In the courtyard, Daniel embraced Laban. "I must go now to the fields. Do return to us, my brother."

Joses emerged from the hill, brushing dust from his clothing.

Laban could not yet leave. When Joses approached, he asked. "May I speak with you?"

Joses seemed not surprised. He turned to Daniel and said, "Say your farewell and be on your way. Tell the men I follow."

Daniel and Laban embraced again. Daniel repeated his invitation, his grin as wide as his face. He loped to the garden gate. He waved, the gate swinging closed behind him.

Joses looked around. Sarah worked at the fire. Her sisters were already at their daily chores. "Let us walk together down the hill," he said to Laban.

When they were on the path that narrowed down to the brush hiding the road below he asked, "How may I help you, Laban?"

"May I join the people of The Way who come here to speak of Jesus?"

"All are welcome, Laban. Come the day after the Sabbath. We will meet then in the courtyard."

Laban took a deep breath. Calling on courage deep within, words rushed from him, "I wish to take Rebekah as my wife. To win her, I will indenture myself to you for as long as you ask, as I have nothing else to offer. I fear that I will no longer be welcome in the house of my father when I tell him I have become one of The Way. I will work in the fields. I will do whatever you ask."

Joses laughed and slapped Laban on the back. "We do not have slaves in this household. And I am certain Rebekah would bring to me much grief if I were to treat you in such a way. Come, son. Let us return to the courtyard. We will sit and speak with Sarah. Later I will go with you to the house of your father."

As they climbed up the hill, Joses patted Laban's back. "Welcome Laban. Welcome to the house of the Lord."

EPILOGUE

The Book Of Anne

Angels appeared to the Nazarene farmer Joachim, foretelling of a birthing by his wife, saying it would be a girl child who would be blessed among all women. There was much celebration in the house of Joachim. When she was born they named her Mary.

The child grew to woman and was betrothed to Joseph of the house of David. While still in the house of Joachim, the angel Gabriel appeared to Mary, saying she carried in her womb the child of God – a boy child whom she would name Emmanuel.

In a dream, a voice coming from a cloud told Joseph, her betrothed, to take her as his wife so that no earthly dishonor would come to the child of God. Angels sang at the child's birth in the town of Bethlehem. Many people bearing gifts came to see him and to proclaim him the Messiah.

Herod the Great heard of the birth of a new king of the Jews and commanded his soldiers to find the child. Joseph, Mary and Jesus fled to Egypt in the arms of angels.

Upon the death of Herod, an angel spoke to Joseph in a dream, commanding him to leave Egypt and return to Israel. Joseph, upon arriving in Jerusalem, decided to take his family to Galilee to live with the family of Mary in the house of Joachim in the Nazarene hills. There they kept the child safely hidden.

During the Passover festival in Jerusalem, when the boy was twelve years of age, Jesus made known to the Temple priests his great knowledge of Scripture. From that time until the days of his preaching, he lived quietly in the village of Nazareth.

This is the story spoken by Anne, mother of Mary, the mother of Jesus. Inscribed here by Laban of Nazareth.

AKNOWLEDGEMENT

My gratitude to:

Harry Ericson for technical advice, research assistance, and loving support.

Jeff Signorini and Alyssa Premru of jsGrafx Creative Services for technical assistance and their design and layout work.

Cathy Foley, Susan Dvornik, and Mark Turley for unceasing encouragement.

Members of the Palm Harbor Writer's Group of Palm Harbor, Florida for "lending their ears" and for offering sage critiques.

To all my friends who encouraged me to complete the book.

Sandy

Made in the USA
Charleston, SC
30 September 2013